Eleanor

by

Audrey Harrison

Published by Audrey Harrison

Copyright 2015 Audrey Harrison

Audrey Harrison asserts the moral right to be identified as the author of this work.

This novel is entirely a work of fiction. The names, characters and incidents portrayed in it are the work of the author's imagination. Any resemblance to actual persons, living or dead, events or localities is entirely coincidental.

This eBook is licensed for your personal enjoyment only. This eBook may not be re-sold or given away to other people.

Thank you for respecting the hard work of this author.

*

This book was proof read by Joan Kelley. Read more about Joan at the end of this story but if you need her, you may reach her at oh1kelley@gmail.com.

Prologue

Joseph Heaton flopped on the vacant chair near Archie Brinklow. "Good God, is there no escape from this inane nonsense, Brinklow? Yet another week of tedium ahead of us," he groaned, much to his friend's amusement.

Archie smiled at Joseph; they had grown up together, their families being linked from one of the many intermarriages that occurred in the ton. His relation and friend sprawled across the chair, his dress perfect as always. Only the best tailor, boot maker and valet for Joseph Heaton. His breeches were a pale buff, fitting his solid legs closely. His waistcoat was characteristically flamboyant, of a pale blue patterned silk, with a darker blue frock coat showing his broad shoulders off to perfection. His boots gleamed, as always, and his cravat stood out in contrast against his waistcoat and frock coat. His black hair was slightly longer than normal, giving ladies the false impression he was of the romantic poetic kind. Archie had known Joseph long enough to know there was not a poetic bone in Joseph's body; he was far too practical and possibly callous but with a handsome face, angled features and a brown-eyed brooding stare ladies would chase him for that alone without the title and fortune that was his.

"Is there no one tempting you?" Archie asked. He was far more easy-going than his friend, equally as well dressed but without Joseph's handsome features, wit and sarcasm. His features were not of the normal sharpness of the aristocracy but more rounded. He still received attention from the ladies, being considered attractive with his blue eyes and brown hair, whereas Joseph was considered one of the finest specimens in society.

"No one I would be willing to tie myself to for the next fifty years at any rate," Joseph responded. "Whoever teaches these girls the art of flirtation should be shot. If I hear one more giggle followed by the fluttering of a fan, I swear I will slap the chit." Why he could not have a civil conversation with any eligible female, he would never know, but if they thought their behaviour was tempting, they were sadly mistaken.

"It will certainly add to your reputation of notoriety," Archie responded with a smirk.

"It won't put off the fortune hunters though."

"It would help if you decided what you're looking for in a wife," Archie said. "One day, you want a tall blonde, the next you want a small brunette; how on earth will you find someone when you change your requirements daily?"

Joseph grinned, his smile lightening his features and turning handsome into beautiful. "I'm keeping my options open," he said with a shrug. He had agreed to marry soon; his ailing mother, whom he adored, had expressed a desire to see her first born and only surviving child settled. At seven and twenty, he was happy to oblige, especially if it meant he could then avoid the marriage mart for the rest of his days. The problem was, having made the decision, he had met no one who tempted him in the slightest.

"What do you really want in a wife?" Archie asked, curious to meet the woman who would tame his friend.

"Beauty, intelligence, educated, a good dancer, sturdy constitution and the ability to make me laugh; in addition to that I want her to know when to be quiet and leave me to do as I wish," Joseph said flippantly.

"Such a small list of requirements; I'm surprised you have not a huge line of eligible women to choose from," Archie said with a raise of his eyebrow.

Joseph laughed bitterly, "I am seriously thinking of paying a respectable looking lightskirt to fool my mother into thinking I'm married and then the poor woman can die in peace. You would think I could give her this one wish, wouldn't you? But as much as I want to please my mother, I am not tying myself to any of the chits being paraded this season."

Archie shook his head, "Your mother would detect an imposter at a hundred paces: she's a lady who has class and sophistication oozing out of every pore; you would never find a lightskirt who could fool her."

Joseph sighed, "I know, or I would do have done it sooner," he admitted.

Archie's butler interrupted them, bringing in a letter, which Archie opened and skimmed through. "It's from West," Archie said. "Ha! He is in Bath, chasing an heiress. Here! Read this; he sounds smitten."

Joseph took the offered letter and read quickly through its contents. He shook his head when he had finished reading. "West will never get anywhere, because he has not listened to a thing I've tried to teach him over the years."

"I dread to ask the question, but what's that?" Archie asked.

"It's very simple," Joseph said, leaning back in his chair, putting his hands behind his head and crossing his ankles in a superior gesture. "The moment you start to chase a girl, she has the advantage and can play you like the smitten fool you are. Pretending nonchalance and indifference is the way to secure her."

"Unless someone who does pander to her gets in there first," Archie said reasonably.

"No, no, my friend; every woman likes a challenge, and she likes to be admired by everyone. If she is not getting attention from one particular gentleman that is the gentleman she wants."

"It can't be that simple," Archie said doubtfully.

"It is, but West has got an even bigger advantage than he realises; the fool probably isn't using it though," Joseph said derisively.

"I'm all ears; tell me of his mistakes," Archie laughed.

"There is a friend," Joseph said simply. "He mentions Lady Lydia and a Miss Johnson. The beautiful Lady Lydia is residing in Bath, so she is at a disadvantage."

"How?"

"Mother has begged me to go to Bath; there are more women than men there apparently," Joseph said with a sneer. "My parent fails to realise it is not lack of beauties we suffer from; it is a severe shortage of quality rather than quantity that is the problem."

"So, how does that affect West's situation?"

"If this Lady Lydia has any sense, she will surround herself with ugly friends. The uglier the better," Joseph said knowledgeably. "If the odds are so to your disadvantage, you have to present yourself to full advantage; therefore, surround yourself with people who show off your beauty even more."

"A little like you do?" Archie said drily.

"Of course," Joseph said good-naturedly. "West should be befriending the ugly friends. He will appear all the better for it in his beauty's eyes. She will fall for the ploy and the man in the process."

"And the friend?" Archie asked.

"Will be realistic about her chances; ugly people are not oblivious to their looks. She will have a few weeks of having the attention of a handsome man before returning to her wallflower status," Joseph responded with conviction.

"Good God, man, that's a cold way to go about things!" Archie said, slightly shocked Joseph would consider using a young lady in such a way. Archie could never act falsely: he did not have the intelligence to do so; if he tried to act as Joseph advised, the result would be marriage to the ugly friend, of that there could be no doubt.

"It's the way of the world, my friend," Joseph said authoritatively.

"What about just liking someone for who they are and showing it?" Archie asked; he had always presumed it would be simple once he found his own life partner, and the thought of having to play deep games frightened him.

"And get yourself trampled in the process? Or worse, used to gain the affection of another? Believe me, women play that game just as much as men do," Joseph said. He had the emotional scars to prove it, but there was no gain in admitting something that had occurred almost as soon as he had left college.

"It involves too many people for it to work in my humble opinion," Archie said, not liking that people could use each other in such a way.

"This is why West and yourself are always floundering and are at risk of being snared by the scheming mamas out there; you don't listen," Joseph said with derision. "As I am such a kind friend, I suggest we take a trip to Bath and guide West through; he's bound to be making a hash of things."

"And you are doing this purely for altruistic reasons?" Archie asked, his tone fully disbelieving.

"It will provide a diversion from this tedious round of engagements," Joseph said. "And you never know; I may fall in love with Lady Lydia myself."

Archie shook his head. There was no point arguing; Joseph was definitely the leader of the three of them. Archie knew he did not have the intelligence to compete with the likes of Joseph; most of the time he was happy to follow his friends' lead. In some ways he regretted mentioning the letter at all: it was going to be difficult if Joseph did fall in love with Lady Lydia; Percy would not take kindly to Joseph wooing the Lady, although Archie had to admit she did sound delightful.

All Archie wanted to do was look-out for a wife of his own. He would have much rather remained in London to secure one of the pretty debutantes, his list of the requirements for a wife far less demanding than Joseph's. He sighed to himself: he might find someone in Bath; one could always hope, but with Joseph around one would also always be at a disadvantage.

Chapter 1

Bath 1819

Eleanor rested her chin on her upturned hand and gazed at her reflection in the looking glass. She sighed. It did not matter how long she looked at herself or which way she turned her head—this way or that—she would never detect beauty in her countenance. She was plain.

Friends and family said she was personable, intelligent, and compassionate, someone they loved without reservation, but she had never stirred any feelings other than friendship in any of the wide acquaintance she had. At twenty she was convinced that the only way to get a husband was to rely on her dowry. She would never receive a marriage proposal from one who loved her for herself.

Those thoughts resulted in another sigh escaping her lips. No matter how much she tried to be stoic about it, she longed to be the focus of someone's life, to feel loved and cherished as Lydia was.

Lady Lydia Moore, her friend, whom Eleanor had met at finishing school and loved deeply, but sometimes—just sometimes—Eleanor wished Lydia appreciated what she had. Lydia was the blonde haired, blue eyed beauty everyone flocked around. She was slightly built, not very tall, which brought out the protective instinct in every man they met. She had a laugh that could only be described as a tinkle and the ability to flirt and banter with the most hardened rake. Added to which, a reasonable fortune and a title, ensured Lydia would make a wonderful match one day. Lydia at twenty was single because she had turned down half a dozen serious offers and numerous silly ones. Eleanor was single because she had yet to receive any offers.

Eleanor was not jealous of Lydia; she would defend her friend to the ends of the world, but sometimes she wished she was not quite so plain in comparison. Eleanor was dark haired, not mysteriously black, just an uninteresting dark brown. Her eyes of green-blue could not decide which colour to be, and her mouth was ordinary, no pouting rosebud lips: she had full lips that were quick to smile, but they would never inspire sonnets to be written about them. Her height and larger build than Lydia made her look even larger than she was when standing next to her friend. But whatever the differences Eleanor would never change their relationship.

Lydia's mother had become ill during the last term at the finishing school they were attending. Lydia had received a letter from her family, explaining, although it was not ideal, the family were going to have an extended visit to Bath. Lydia had asked Eleanor to accompany them, and Eleanor had happily agreed to the scheme. A return home would only see Eleanor forced into a marriage with a stranger. Having only daughters, her father wished all his girls to marry someone with a title, or if not, marry the man he had chosen to take over his business and keep it in the family when he became too old to continue.

Eleanor came with a large fortune, as her other sisters before her did, but she was ultimately the daughter of a 'cit', a man of business, so was not very appealing to most of the aristocracy. Her two eldest sisters, Rosalind and Annabelle, had married titled men, Rosalind becoming a Duchess and Annabelle, a Lady, having married Lord Stannage the Earl of Garston, which left Grace and herself. Grace was staying with Rosalind and, by all accounts, Rosalind was doing everything she could to match make. Eleanor had not met the man who was helping to run her father's business but had received unfavourable reports from the sisters who had. If Grace married a titled gentleman, it would be down to Eleanor to marry Mr Wadeson, a thought that did not appeal to her, although she was resigned that at least she would be married.

All of her sisters had grown up with the desire to have large families; their parents had not been neglectful in providing for their daughters, but they had been remiss where attention and love had been concerned. Rosalind, the eldest, had been a substitute mother, and they had thrived under her care, but it reinforced the urge they all shared: a need to have children of their own.

Eleanor and Lydia had only been settled a few weeks, and already they were fully involved in the social whirl that was Bath. Lydia was, as expected, surrounded by potential beaux, and Eleanor provided friendly support for those who wanted to get closer to Lydia but were trampled in the crush of the more experienced gentlemen.

"Mirror, mirror on the wall, I don't want to be the fairest of them all, but couldn't you spare just one Prince Charming?" Eleanor grinned at her reflection as the looking glass remained quiet. "I suppose Bath isn't full of Princes at this time of year, so I shall forgive you this poor performance this time, but don't make a habit of it." She pulled a face at herself before leaving the room; there was no use pining after something that would not happen.

*

The weekly ball at the Lower Assembly Rooms was always a crush. Eleanor and Lydia squeezed through the crowd, Lydia leading the way.

"They must be here somewhere." she muttered to Eleanor over her shoulder, her cheeks glowing at the rising heat.

"Lydia, they will have look-outs in wait for you." Eleanor teased.

Lydia grinned, "I don't want to waste a moment of the evening; we only have until eleven."

Eleanor smiled in return; Lydia would dance all night, if allowed, but in Bath it was the Master of Ceremonies who dictated the time they went home.

Very soon, they were hailed by one of Lydia's admirers, and Lydia relaxed. She always doubted her enjoyment until she saw a familiar face and then was assured a good night. Eleanor joined in the greetings; Mr Percy West was the most successful of Lydia's admirers since their arrival in Bath. Eleanor liked him; he seemed to understand Lydia more than her other beaux. Although Lydia showed preference to him in public, in private, Eleanor could not find out if it were a serious attachment on Lydia's part.

Mr West made his greetings and then introduced his friends who had been holding back a little. "Ladies, may I introduce Mr Joseph Heaton and Mr Archie Brinklow? Gentlemen, this is Lady Lydia Moore and Miss Johnson. Bath has been a brighter place since Lady Lydia joined its company."

Joseph raised his eyes to the ceiling. It was obvious Percy was making a bungle of things. Joseph would never have offered a compliment to one young lady, while leaving out another. To her credit the friend seemed to take the faux-pas in her stride, the only outward sign she had registered the omission was the smallest of smiles on her lips. He resolved to have a word with his friends and try to prevent causing offence wherever they went.

Lydia dimpled under the compliment from Mr West and held out her hand in turn to the gentlemen. Eleanor saw with a wry smile both were instantly smitten by her friend. To Mr Brinklow's credit and Mr West's chagrin the former gentleman secured the first two dances with Lydia immediately.

"Well, I say, Brinklow! That's mighty unsporting of you," Mr West spluttered as Lydia accepted the request for dances.

"If you wanted the honour West, you should have secured this gem before making the introductions." Mr Brinklow smiled at Lydia. "I would never have been so foolish." Archie had shocked himself with his ungentlemanly behaviour, but Eleanor had guessed correctly: one look at Lady Lydia and Archie had been smitten. Her blonde ringlets seemed to frame her face, making her look positively angelic. Her blue eyes had sparkled up at him, and he had been lost. Percy would have to look out for himself: Archie was in love. All his commendable thoughts of allowing Percy to chase the Lady Lydia unheeded had gone out of the window; Archie was besotted within seconds.

Lydia preened, "Don't worry, Mr West, I shall secure the next two for you if you like," she soothed.

"I should be delighted," Mr West bowed, slightly mollified.

Lydia and Mr Brinklow moved off to the dancefloor as the instruments started to prepare.

"Another one is led willingly into the lair," Eleanor said softly to herself as she noticed the smitten look on Mr Brinklow's face.

"I'm sure he'll survive." came a quiet voice at her side.

Eleanor jumped; she had not meant anyone to overhear. Turning she saw Mr Heaton smiling slightly at her, a teasing expression in his eyes. Eleanor laughed, "I'm sure he will, but he may not come away unscathed; there are a multitude of bodies left behind in every town Lady Lydia visits."

"In that case I feel I should remain close to my friend in order to step in if he is in danger. Would you do the honour of having the next dance with me Miss Johnson?"

Eleanor inclined her head in acquiescence. This one was good, she acknowledged as they joined the same set; he would spend nearly as much time with Lydia as Mr Brinklow. Eleanor silently congratulated his good judgement; if he then followed Mr West with two dances he would spend more time with Lydia than any of the other men.

Joseph was congratulating himself on exactly the same thing. It had all gone exactly to plan in his opinion; he was dancing with the friend, who as it turned out was quite pleasing to the eye, not nearly as ugly as he had anticipated.

The dance started and, as Eleanor and Joseph were the bottom couple, she had a chance to speak to this newcomer.

"Are you in Bath long, Mr Heaton?" she asked.

"We've come down to allow Brinklow to rusticate a little; West extended his hospitality, and we are quite comfortable at his house, "Joseph explained; it was an acceptable story and avoided any mention of titles or the aims of the men with regards to marriage.

Eleanor knew Mr West to have hired a house in Queens Square, not the most popular address in town, but more than suitable for a single man. "It's a good spot to be: close to everything but near enough to escape to the outlying areas as well."

"I suppose so; I had never thought about it in that way, but I can see the appeal. Do you often need to escape?" Joseph asked; it was a curious term to be used by a young lady.

"Me? No! I am too busy with Lady Lydia's activities to have time for escape; she has boundless energy and even more appointments." Eleanor explained with a laugh.

"I can imagine." Anyone who set eyes on Lydia would hardly be able to do anything other than spend time in her company; she was clearly the prettiest girl in Bath.

Eleanor assessed the gentleman standing before her: he was obviously quieter than the other two of their group; he had held back a little during their introductions. Eleanor did not think this was from any lack of confidence; he seemed very sure of himself: calm, confident and somehow a little unnerving. When he looked at Eleanor, she felt as if he could see into her soul.

She had no further time for reflection as the set moved down, and they joined the dance.

"You dance very well, Miss Johnson," Joseph said as they joined hands on a turn.

"You compliment even better." Eleanor replied with a teasing smile.

"Do I not gain favour by my flattery?" he asked with a twinkle in his eyes; her retorts amused him.

"I'm always willing to be flattered, but I would wonder why you wish to gain favour."

"If I gain favour with you, you would perhaps be more willing to look kindly on a newcomer to the area," came the reply on the next turn.

"As you are one of a handsome trio, I doubt very much you will be lacking in invitations or entertainments," Eleanor responded with a smile.

"A compliment, and on such short acquaintance; I am honoured," Joseph teased with a raise of an eyebrow.

"I am stating the truth; please don't run away with my words and pretend I am trying to flatter you in order to gain favour with you, Mr Heaton!" she teased playfully.

"I would not be so vain," Joseph said with a smile, but he wondered if he were. At every opportunity he took the words of those around him as flattery: his partner's words made him pause; she certainly did not seem to be wishing to flatter him. In fact, he had the distinct impression she was laughing at him. "You dance divinely, Miss Johnson, and I hope you will take that compliment as the truth and not one offered with empty flattery in mind."

Eleanor glowed a little, a real compliment, and she liked it. She bowed her head in acquiesce. "I am not foolish enough to refuse a sincere compliment Mr Heaton; none of us is so confident as to do that."

Joseph smiled at his partner in appreciation, and they continued to enjoy the dance.

Chapter 2

Lydia danced with the three men and then moved on to other acquaintances. Eleanor enjoyed watching her friend; she really was a beautiful girl. She took pride in the way people looked at her as she danced. The men openly admired her; the women looked on enviously. She had no idea who would finally win her friend's heart but was aware that Lydia's parents were hoping their daughter would marry soon.

Eleanor sat at the edge of the assembly room. It was extremely hot, and she found a seat where the breeze from the open windows entered the room. She did not dance every dance at any assembly but especially at ones where the women outnumbered the men as was the case on this particular evening.

Mr Heaton approached her with a smile on his face. Eleanor thought privately Lydia should concentrate on Mr Heaton: handsome, his hair was a black that seemed darker than the night. His face was smooth, but had the sharp aristocratic jaw and nose of the ton, with low brows over gleaming eyes. Always in fashion, his was the smooth boyish face of the poet that made the ladies swoon but, to Eleanor, he looked like an Adonis. He was a tall, broad man; she had appreciated his height whilst dancing with him. It was always gratifying to dance with someone who was not dwarfed by her own height. She pondered the way he moved; it was with a confidence more usual in an aristocrat than a mere gentleman.

She returned his smile as he sat next to her on the bench. There was very little room, and Eleanor almost caught her breath as his leg brushed hers. She was quick to gather herself, though; she had no patience with silliness, especially her own.

"Not dancing, Mr Heaton?" she asked pleasantly.

"I was just about to ask you the same question," Joseph responded with a smile; he had been drawn to her as soon as he noticed her alone. It was, of course, part of his ploy, but he did not consciously think that when he saw her; he had just been drawn to her.

"No, sometimes it is best to sit out rather than have a pity dance," Eleanor whispered conspiratorially.

"A pity dance?" he asked, looking confused.

"Yes, one in which some poor soul knows Lady Lydia's parents and, out of pity, is forced to dance with the daughter of a 'cit'," Eleanor explained with a mischievous smile. "Sometimes I can dance for a full half hour without conversation: business acumen could be catching, Mr Heaton; you had better beware!"

Joseph laughed in genuine amusement at her words. "They dislike you because of your father's trade? The fact you are here would suggest he is a successful businessman?"

"He is; in fact, he has been able to provide his four daughters with large dowries," Eleanor responded lightly.

Joseph wondered if she were letting him know she was available and rich; he felt slight disappointment at her unsubtlety. Just when he thought she must be, she spoke as if reading his mind. "Don't worry, Mr Heaton; I'm not parading my wares as if I am a horse at Tattersall's: I'm just being honest. I am not looking for a husband."

"Isn't that the aim of every young lady?" Joseph asked, a little surprised at her directness, but he had to admit to himself he liked her direct way.

"I would imagine so, but there is so much strain put on a perfectly good friendship because one of the party lives in fear that one wrong move and they will be leg-shackled to a person they only like. That would not be the way to secure a marriage; it would be purgatory." Eleanor said with feeling. She was letting him know she was not hoping to secure him, but she knew he would not consider her in any case; someone as attractive and charismatic as he would have his pick of society even without a title. She would be fooling herself if she considered the thought for a moment that someone as handsome and confident as he would consider a Plain Jane; that was her lot.

Joseph frowned and opened his mouth to speak, but he closed it again and just smiled in acknowledgement of the comment. Any further conversation was interrupted by Lydia's approach.

"Mr Heaton, Eleanor, why are you skulking here?" Lydia asked, waving her fan frantically. "It is time for tea. I hope you would be good enough to escort us, Mr Heaton?"

"I would be delighted," Joseph said smoothly, rising and offering the two ladies his arms.

"Good! I've told Mr West and Mr Brinklow to secure us a table and refreshments," Lydia said as they made their way through the throng.

It was only a short way between the ball room and the tea room, but the mass of people moving together made progress slow. Lydia chatted easily as they ambled.

"I hope you will join us tomorrow for breakfast in Sydney Gardens? It would be a poor show if you didn't," Lydia said. "Mr West always escorts us, doesn't he Eleanor?"

"He does," Eleanor acknowledged. "But perhaps we shouldn't presume Mr Heaton will attend; he could be otherwise engaged." Sometimes Eleanor wished Lydia were a little more reserved. Her own natural politeness was shocked at Lydia's forthright manner to virtual strangers.

Eleanor was to find once again that Lydia did not offend when Mr Heaton spoke. "As both Brinklow and I are residing with Mr West, we had presumed we would take part in any entertainment he does. It would be a pleasure to join you for breakfast tomorrow. I'm sure Mr West will have no objections in us accompanying him, "came the unruffled reply.

"I'm not so sure he won't have objections; three to one are not very good odds even for the most confident of beaux," Eleanor could not resist muttering. She was sure Lydia had not heard, but the coughing fit Mr Heaton suffered immediately after she spoke made her suspicious her caustic tongue had been overheard by him at least.

After supper, the remainder of the evening was spent with other acquaintances. Lydia was always careful not to give the gossips anything to talk about. It was only when they had been deposited by the sedan chairs at their address on Henrietta Street that Eleanor could question Lydia about the evening.

"Mr West is becoming very attached to you." Eleanor said as she brushed out her friend's hair. It was a nightly ritual, one that Eleanor enjoyed; Lydia's hair was soft, long and fell in natural waves.

"I haven't given him any encouragement," Lydia said, a little defensively. "I only danced with him twice."

"Mr Brinklow is a handsome man," Eleanor said, trying to off-set the mood that could so easily be brought on sometimes.

"He is, as is Mr Heaton," Lydia replied. "It's nice to have more gentleman join our society. Bath has been quite limiting."

Eleanor smiled at her friend through the mirror; she had not sat out one dance since their arrival, but yet she found the society limiting. Most young ladies would be delighted at such attention, but not Lydia.

"Well, you shall have all three dancing attendance tomorrow at breakfast," Eleanor reassured Lydia as she finished brushing her hair. "I'm sure they will be fighting for your attention once more."

*

Eleanor and Lydia strolled down Great Pulteney Street arm in arm, both young ladies anticipating the joys of the public breakfast. Lydia was looking forward to seeing her three conquests from the previous evening, while Eleanor was looking forward to spending the morning in the gardens. She had quickly fallen in love with Bath; it was far more relaxed than London. A single woman was not so much out of place as they were in the capital city, so Eleanor felt more at ease.

The friends were not escorted by a maid or footman. Lydia's parents looked on Eleanor as more of a companion than another woman also looking for a husband even though she was the same age as their daughter. Her more serious manner lulled them into allowing her the extra responsibility.

Mr West was waiting at the gates to Sydney Gardens. His face lit up when he saw Lydia approaching, and both young ladies smiled in greeting.

"Good morning Lady Lydia, Miss Johnson. It's a fine day for our breakfast," Mr West greeted the pair with a bow. "If you would care to take my arm, I will happily lead you to our spot."

Both ladies accepted the offer, and Eleanor suppressed a smile. Mr West was obviously not taking any chances Mr Brinklow would take the lead this morning. They walked through the groups of others gathering for the public breakfast. Lydia spotted Mr Brinklow as he waved to draw their attention. A table had been secured, and waiters were supplying tea, Bath buns and other delights.

The two gentlemen rose to greet the ladies and bowed their good mornings. They were both dressed in the height of fashion: dark frock coats, snug waistcoats and breeches. The white of their collars and cravats contrasted against their skin but none so much as Mr Heaton's. The darker hue of his skin made the contrast more pronounced. Eleanor tore her eyes away; she could not spend all day staring, however tempting a proposition it was.

Eleanor was seated between Mr West and Mr Brinklow, Lydia seated between Mr Brinklow and Mr Heaton. Eleanor stifled a smile; Mr West had looked put-out at his position but, unsurprisingly, the other two gentlemen seemed perfectly content.

Lydia turned to Joseph, her blue eyes large and round fluttering up at him. "So, Mr Heaton, what pleasures can we tempt you with to keep you entertained in Bath?"

"I am sure that anything involving you would give me more than enough pleasure," Joseph answered quickly, smiling down at the young woman.

"I may involve you in all sorts of outings; after all you have just given me free rein," Lydia smiled, looking at the Adonis through her lashes.

"I'm sure I would cope if the company is as pleasant as it is now. With yourself and Miss Johnson to entertain us, what more could we ask for?" Joseph saw Eleanor raise an eyebrow at him, and he suppressed a smile. "What is it, Miss Johnson? Do you not wish for our company?"

"I was appreciating your compliments, Mr Heaton, nothing more," Eleanor responded, but she gave a glare in Joseph's direction before masking her expression once more with a smile, letting him know she would always be able to offer a retort even though he might test her.

"Eleanor is very patient with me," Lydia confided. "I do not have a dearer friend. I could not be in Bath without her; my parents would drive me to distraction!"

"A true friend is certainly very dear, and I am sure that Miss Johnson is enjoying her sojourn in this city," Mr Heaton replied.

"More and more," Eleanor responded with a smile, which convinced Joseph his flirting techniques were being mocked, which surprisingly made him want to have Miss Johnson's approval rather than her censure.

Percy decided his friend had held the attention of his chosen one for long enough and interrupted the conversation. "Lady Lydia, do not forget we have a phaeton ride planned this afternoon; I thought we might visit Bradford-on-Avon? I have been reliably informed there is a pretty little tea shop near the river."

"Yes, that would be lovely; Eleanor is insisting on remaining in the gardens," Lydia said.

"All day?" Joseph asked.

"I like to walk, but Lydia doesn't share that interest," Eleanor said amenably.

"In that case, why don't myself and Mr Brinklow accompany you on your walk?" Joseph said, not wishing to miss an opportunity in which he could find out exactly why he was so obviously being teased.

"Why don't we hire a phaeton and accompany Lady Lydia? I could ride, and you could drive Miss Johnson," Mr Brinklow said quickly.

Joseph immediately saw what his friend was trying to do; if Archie was on horseback, he would spend the journey as close to the phaeton carrying Lady Lydia as he could. From the expression on Percy's face, he knew exactly what Archie was trying to do as well.

Eleanor thought it prudent to interrupt before any more of her day was disrupted. "Why don't you both travel on horseback, thus preventing the cost of hiring a phaeton, and I can continue my day as I planned?" She tried to keep the sharpness out of her voice but was not convinced she had achieved it.

"Oh, but, Eleanor, it would make the day more pleasurable if you joined us," Lydia said with feeling.

"And you would not need a different chaperone," Eleanor said, this time her sharpness coming through. She normally did not mind being classed as chaperone, but she did not wish to be so openly used.

"Brinklow, I don't wish for a ride: a stretch of the legs is far more preferable to me this fine day; we should leave a phaeton ride for another day," Joseph said diplomatically. He had seen Eleanor's annoyance and quickly responded to soothe her. They were there pandering to Lady Lydia, but Joseph would not continue when their actions were causing someone else discomfort. He failed to realise that previously he had done exactly that when playing the game of romance, but for some reason he had reacted as a result of seeing Miss Johnson's discomfort.

Archie knew when to admit defeat, so he did not argue against Joseph's words. The stern stare he received was enough to convey Joseph's feelings on the matter, and the subject was dropped.

The ladies separated from the gentlemen and returned to their lodgings, Lydia wishing to change for her phaeton ride and Eleanor needing to put on her boots for walking and to collect her maid to accompany her. She had arranged to meet Mr Heaton and Mr Brinklow with mixed feelings, which she tried to dismiss. Having company would mean she could walk further. If Mr Brinklow was there under duress, she was not about to repine; Lydia was quite welcome to all three gentlemen. Well, perhaps there was one of the three Eleanor would have enjoyed a flirtation with but, as no wonderful transformation had occurred overnight to turn Eleanor into an astounding beauty, she would put on her boots and enjoy a walk with two of Lydia's beaux.

Chapter 3

The threesome walked onto the canal bank with the maid trailing behind at a suitable distance. It was a relatively new addition that cut through the Sydney Gardens. It was made for practicalities: transporting goods more efficiently, but there was a gate from the gardens enabling access to anyone wishing to walk the towpath.

Eleanor had wished to explore along the path but had not felt it was appropriate with only herself and Lydia. The people working the canal boats did not worry her, but Lydia had been shocked when the men had cat-called to them when they stood watching the boats one day over the canal bridge.

Archie looked questioningly at Joseph when Eleanor suggested they take a walk on the tow path, but Joseph shrugged and followed the young lady. It was her walk, and he could see no real problems, although his valet might not feel the same nonchalance when he presented his muddy boots to him later.

They stood to one side as a horse and its master pulled a boat full of coal past them. A woman and young girl sat at the rear of the boat. Joseph had turned to recommence the walk when the voice of the older woman rang out behind them.

"Er, love, when ye gets sick of 'er prim and proper ways, come and find me; I'll show 'e a good time!" The words were finished with a cackle of laughter, which followed them as the boat glided around a bend in the canal.

"Disgraceful talk in front of a lady!" Archie spluttered.

Eleanor laughed, "Don't be angry on my account, Mr Brinklow: she was only funning you; there was no harm done."

Joseph raised an eyebrow, "What, not swooning into a fainting fit at her suggestion?"

"Hardly!" Eleanor snorted. "I've spent time in one of my father's mills. I learned a whole new vocabulary on the day I donned a rough cotton pinafore and walked through with one of the more welcoming foremen. Rosalind nearly had a heart attack when she found out."

Joseph laughed at the thought of Eleanor trying to blend in with the factory girls. She would have stood out like a rose in a garden of weeds; the girls were probably swearing more than normal to try and shock her. "Who is Rosalind?" he asked.

"My eldest sister, lately the Duchess of Sudworth; she cared for myself and my two other older sisters when we were growing up. The consequence of parents more interested in things other than their children," Eleanor said simply. They might find her words shockingly honest, but she did not see the point of trying to hide the truth.

"The Duchess of Sudworth," Joseph said. "Your father must have been very pleased at the connection."

"He arranged it," Eleanor said with derision. "Poor Rosalind had met the Duke only once prior to her marriage; he was penniless and, as I've said before, we come with large dowries, and father was happy to pay handsomely for such a grand title."

Joseph was astounded she was so open about her family business; this was definitely not the thing to do in polite society but, instead of condemning her for it, he silently applauded her. It was refreshing to have someone speak so honestly, although he had to suppress a smile at Archie's shocked face.

"What did your sister feel about the situation? Was she happy with the title?" Joseph could not resist probing. For the first time since he had left the schoolroom, he felt as if he was in the company of a direct woman, and he liked it.

"She was as angry as I've ever seen her, but there was no dissuading Father, so the marriage went ahead. She has been very fortunate; although not a love match at the start, it is now. Her letters are full of her husband and how wonderful he is," Eleanor said with a smile. "I've not met him, but I am inclined to like him, for he appears to be making Rosalind happy."

"The Duke of Sudworth? He's a decent man; the family have had a hard time of it over the last few years," Archie responded.

"Oh, do you know him? Rosalind seemed to suggest he doesn't like London so much," Eleanor said, curious to learn more about the new addition to her family.

Joseph gave Archie a warning look, which had the desired effect. "Oh, I don't know him that well, just through reputation really," Archie backtracked quickly.

"I shall meet him sometime soon, I am sure; all my sisters are due to visit Rosalind in their turn," Eleanor said vaguely. There was no advantage in explaining how ruthless her father was about his daughters gaining marriage partners. Her conversation had already been inappropriate for such a newly acquired acquaintance even though she felt perfectly at ease with Mr Heaton. Surprisingly so, but she was not prepared to delve into why she felt so comfortable with him.

Eleanor had increased Joseph's curiosity with her words. There was clearly a complicated family behind her flippancy, but she seemed to be perfectly at ease with that fact. All too often he saw young men and women who were cowed by a tyrant of a father, or mother come to that; he was reassured to see she was not, seeming level-headed and open.

They returned to Sydney Gardens along the same pathway and stopped for refreshments. Eleanor felt quite decadent being escorted by two handsome gentlemen; it did not happen enough in her opinion, she smiled to herself.

"What mischief are you thinking now, Miss Johnson?" Joseph asked noticing the smile. Archie had gone to speak with someone he knew, so they were alone for the moment.

"I can get away with nothing, can I?" Eleanor said, trying to maintain a stern demeanour and failing.

"As you almost choked me with your mutterings once, I have needed to brace myself near you since," Joseph responded.

"I was just thinking what a pleasant afternoon it is; that is all," Eleanor said airily.

"Hmm, I'm not fully convinced, although to not believe what you say would be very poor of me," Joseph said leaning back in his chair and folding his arms.

"You will just have to be a gentleman and accept what I say then," Eleanor said primly, but there was a twinkle in her eyes and a smile around her lips that off-set the tone of the words.

Archie returned to his seat and smiled at the pair. "That was a friend of my parents; they invited us to a ball tomorrow evening. I told them of our acquaintance with yourself and Lady Lydia, Miss Johnson, and they are going to send an invitation around to your address," Archie said, pleased with himself. He was sure the party would contain mainly older aged friends, which would give himself and his two friends added advantage with regards to Lady Lydia. He had vowed to help Percy, but he was finding that difficult to put into practice when his every waking thought was of a particular blue-eyed beauty.

"I hope we will be able to attend; balls are always a welcome diversion," Eleanor replied.

"Because of your love of dancing?" Joseph asked, sending a look in Archie's direction.

"Oh, I love to dance, but they are a perfect place to watch people," Eleanor responded with a smile. "I perhaps should not admit to it, but I gain a lot of entertainment in watching others."

"We shall have to be on our guard, Archie," Joseph said with a raised eyebrow. "Or our idiosyncrasies will be entertaining Miss Johnson long after our dancing abilities do."

Eleanor laughed, "I cannot deny it, Mr Heaton," she smiled up at him.

Joseph smiled in response, her eyes twinkled when she smiled, the blue seeming to glitter through the green. He had noticed her eyes when they first met, a mixture of green and blue. As he was becoming more acquainted with her, he noticed different emotions produced varying emphasis on her eye colour. It was an intriguing trait, and he watched her all the more closely to see the differing effects.

"In that case, we should make a pact to keep Miss Johnson busy on the dancefloor, what do you say Archie?"

Archie picked up the meaning in Joseph's words and immediately responded. "A capital idea! If I may have the honour of the first two dances with you Miss Johnson?" he asked.

"If we have no other engagements; I'm afraid I am reliant on Lady Moore's approval of the scheme but, if we do attend, I would happily accept your offer," Eleanor responded with a smile.

"And could I have the pleasure of the third and fourth?" Joseph asked, pleased Archie had responded appropriately.

"Of course," Eleanor said, the thought of the third and fourth dances sending an unexpected fluttering to her stomach.

They finished off their refreshments and exchanged a word or two with a few acquaintances Eleanor had formed since arriving in Bath. They walked around to the front of the hotel, and Eleanor thanked the gentlemen for their time, expressing how she had enjoyed the excursion.

"Excellent. Shall we escort you to your lodgings, Miss Johnson?" Joseph asked. They had been out for quite a while; it was appropriate to end their outing.

Eleanor acceded, and they walked back along Great Pulteney Street, the maid the only one who was relieved the afternoon's exertions were coming to an end. The pavement was wide enough to allow them to walk three abreast without causing obstruction to others on the street, the maid once again following behind. Continuing into Laura Place and then turning into Henrietta Street, they stopped at the iron archway leading to number six where Eleanor and the Moore family were staying.

"Thank you for a lovely afternoon," Eleanor said with a curtsey.

"The pleasure was all ours," Joseph responded with a bow that was duplicated by Archie. "Have a pleasant day, Miss Johnson."

Eleanor turned to the house, thinking the day could not possibly be improved.

Joseph and Archie continued over Pulteney Bridge. Percy was staying in a property in Queens Square, not as desirable an address as the area they had just passed through but perfectly acceptable for three gentlemen.

Archie waited until Henrietta Street was far behind them before speaking. "That was a great hint you gave me back there Joseph; I would never have thought of asking Miss Johnson for the first two."

"Why ever not? If you have invited a young lady to a ball, it is only natural you would secure dances with her," Joseph said with a shake of his head. He sometimes worried about Archie; he was too slow to do the right thing.

"I wanted to secure the first two with Lady Lydia, of course; it was I who secured an invitation for them, so I was hoping my reward would be the first two with her, but I saw what you were doing," Archie said happily.

"And that was?" Joseph asked, his voice an amused drawl.

"Making something of the plain friend to gain even more favour with Lady Lydia," Archie said smugly.

Joseph looked at his friend sharply. The anger that hit him at the thought of Miss Johnson being used took him by surprise. That it was only as a result of his own instructions to Archie did not seem to occur to him. "That sounded like an insult to Miss Johnson; I hope it wasn't."

"It wasn't an insult," Archie said quickly. "But you have to admit that Lady Lydia is a beauty."

"She is," Joseph conceded but, for some reason, being told Eleanor was considered plain when compared with her friend rankled him. He shook himself: Lady Lydia was beautiful; Archie meant no harm. Joseph had said to make a fuss of the plain friend, and Miss Johnson was no beauty in comparison to Lady Lydia, but somehow his equilibrium had been upset. "Are you seriously going in competition against Percy for Lady Lydia's affection?" he asked, trying to focus his mind.

"Are you not?" Archie countered. "She is the most delightful creature; it was no wonder Percy raved about her."

"I haven't decided," Joseph responded.

"Ha! That's a yes if ever I heard one!" Archie said with a chuckle. "You don't fool me, Joe. You will encourage me to come to blows with Percy and, while we are distracted, you will move in and collect the spoils for yourself."

"So romantically put," Joseph responded with derision. "If you two fools want to come to blows, I won't be encouraging you or dissuading you. You surprise me Archie; you were quite defensive of Percy's affection before we came, but now you're putting yourself in direct competition with him."

"I know, and I feel like a total cad, but from the moment I laid eyes on her, I was in love," Archie said dreamily.

Joseph wanted to laugh but restrained himself. "In love before finding out her character?"

"This is why you will never feel true love; it isn't rational or considered: it's just a feeling," Archie said dramatically, feeling pity for his friend.

"You will be spouting poetry next," Joseph drawled.

"I might if I am inspired to do so," Archie said huffily. "What is annoying about the whole situation, Joe, is that you may not feel anything long-lasting for Lady Lydia and still you will try to secure her heart."

Joseph looked at his friend in surprise; the thought had not crossed his mind. "I haven't decided what I am to do: you know my view on marriage and love."

"Yes, she's got a title, so she will be indifferent about gaining a title because she already has one; she's no fortune hunter, which we both have suffered from. She has beauty, is a good dancer, is intelligent, just to list a few from your long list of requirements. Need I go on?" Archie responded. His friend had gone over with them all his requirements in a marriage partner for himself and, the more Archie thought about it, the more he was convinced Joseph would pursue Lady Lydia. The thought depressed him even though he was still trying to convince himself he should be a decent friend and promote Percy to Lady Lydia.

The usually calm, confident Joseph actually looked uncomfortable for once. "Damn society," he muttered. He had started on a scheme and now was too far down that road to turn back, yet the thought of remaining focused on what he had said he wanted was suddenly leaving him feeling cold inside.

*

Lydia burst into Eleanor's bedchamber. "Oh, Eleanor, I have had such a lovely day!" she exclaimed, coming into the room and twirling around in the centre.

Eleanor smiled at Lydia, "That's obvious from the look of you; you'd better tell me all about it."

Lydia sat on the edge of Eleanor's bed and waited until Eleanor closed her book. "Mr West declares I'm the finest looking woman in Bath, and he wishes to court me," Lydia said, pretending modesty but beaming at Eleanor.

"You are the finest looking in Bath and beyond, I imagine," Eleanor replied honestly. "Has he spoken to your father?"

"Goodness no! And I've told him in no uncertain terms he mustn't," Lydia said forcefully. "I do not wish to attach myself to him at this stage."

"I don't understand," Eleanor said puzzled. "If you are on your way to being in love with him, why not be attached; you can always have a long engagement."

"What if I met someone I like better?" Lydia asked seriously.

"But if you love someone, you would surely believe there was no one better. You do love him, don't you, Lydia? Surely you wouldn't allow him to court you if you didn't love him?" Eleanor answered with a frown. This was a side to Lydia she had not seen previously.

"There are many men I could love," Lydia explained patiently. "I want to be sure I accept the best proposal I can. Mr West is pleasant; I like him, but I'm not sure his prospects are good enough for me."

Eleanor shook her head at her friend. "I'm not saying accept the first proposal you receive if you don't like the man; I know you have refused other proposals, but if you hesitate in accepting one from someone you do love, you risk losing him if you dally for too long."

"Oh, Eleanor, you are silly; of course, he will wait for me: he is smitten," Lydia responded confidently. "Until I am sure of what other proposals there are, I refuse to give an answer."

"I don't think I would have your confidence; what if he also met someone else?" Eleanor asked.

"Then I give him something that will encourage him to be loyal to me," Lydia replied and started to laugh at Eleanor's shocked expression. "A kiss in private, Eleanor; that is all! I was not referring to anything else!"

"A kiss is enough to compromise you," Eleanor responded. Her sister Annabelle had been compromised in that exact way, so she was speaking with authority.

"Oh, you are such an innocent! Of course, it would be given where there was no chance of us being discovered. I am no fool, and I intend accepting the marriage proposal offering me the best chances in life," Lydia said with a defiant tilt of her head.

Eleanor was surprised and a little shocked at Lydia's outlook. The view of her own father was quite mercenary, but Lydia's view seemed even worse somehow. That a businessman could be calculating about marriage was one thing, but a young woman to be so cynical saddened and shocked her. It was quite a depressing thought that even someone so young could be so calculated about love and marriage. Eleanor began to feel her ideals were outdated and, as a result, felt little lost for the first time in her life.

Chapter 4

Lord and Lady Moore did accept the invitation sent round by the Dowager Divine, Archie's family friend. While Eleanor was waiting for Lydia to finish her toilette, she told her of her dance partners.

"That is excellent!" Lydia said. "And with Mr West, who I'm sure will also dance with you for two, you will hardly be seated at all. You sometimes sit out far too many dances."

Eleanor did not respond that it was more to do with lack of dancing partners than not wishing to dance. Lydia would never understand the concept of a lack of dance partners; it was something she had never experienced.

"It leaves Mr Heaton to take my first two," Lydia replied, applying rouge to her cheeks.

"Will you not be dancing with Mr West?" Eleanor asked.

"Why, of course not!" Lydia laughed. "He would presume too much from it. I think getting to know Mr Heaton and Mr Brinklow better would be best. It means I can see what potential they have while at the same time annoying Mr West enough to keep him very attentive."

"Oh, I see," Eleanor responded dully. The thought of Lydia using Mr Heaton in such a way did not rest easy with her. She soon recollected herself; he was a grown man: it was up to him whether or not he fell for Lydia's charms and calculations.

Both young women dressed to impress their unknown hosts and guests. Lydia opted for a blue satin dress. She often chose to wear varying shades of blue or cream as they showed off her eyes and complexion to their best effect. Eleanor had always thought it was a happy accident that her friend dressed to set-off her attributes to their best, but since her conversation with Lydia about marriage, she was no longer so sure it was an innocent action.

Eleanor dressed in a pale green taffeta dress. She liked earthy colours and, although restricted to the lighter colours because of her age and position as a single woman, she had a wide range to choose from that she liked wearing. The dress was embroidered with deeper green leaves in a very delicate and intricate pattern. A simple chain with emerald droplet was the only jewellery she wore. It was not through lack of owning expensive jewellery that drove her choice, she preferred simpler pieces.

Lord and Lady Moore, along with Eleanor and Lady Lydia entered the large drawing room at the address on The Paragon and were introduced to the assembled guests. The three gentlemen had already arrived but were not the first to make their bows to the new arrivals. Archie had been correct in his assumption that the gathered throng would be more mature in age than themselves, but this did not stop the male residents making a fuss of Lydia the moment they were introduced. The three friends watched the spectacle with differing levels of emotion.

"It appears we are to have unlooked-for competition after all," Joseph drawled with a look in Archie's direction.

"Look at how they are fawning over her!" Percy said with a growl.

"Most of them are old enough to be her father!" Archie snapped, keeping his voice low.

"Not beyond being attracted to a pretty face obviously," Joseph responded, amused at the scowls on his friends' faces.

Eventually Lydia and Eleanor joined the gentlemen. After the exchange of bows and curtseys had taken place, Lydia fluttered her eyes at Joseph. "Mr Heaton, you find me at a disadvantage to Miss Johnson tonight."

"Oh? How so?" Joseph asked, sending an enquiring look to Eleanor. Surprisingly, he saw a forced blank expression, an unusual occurrence for Eleanor. He had until that moment enjoyed watching her emotions flit across her face. He was curious but turned back to Lydia, who was looking at him with round, sad eyes.

"Why, she has secured the first four dances tonight when I haven't got a single one! Now don't you think that is a poor show?" Lydia asked, with a sad smile.

Eleanor gritted her teeth.

"Oh, my dear me, yes," Joseph responded. "Please allow me to have the honour of the first two."

"Oh, if you insist," Lydia sighed, "That is very kind of you; and you, Mr Brinklow, are you to make amends for abandoning me? Shall I keep the next two free?"

"Of course, I would be delighted," Archie responded with a triumphant smile towards Percy.

"And if I could have the next two?" Percy quickly asked, annoyed at his friends that they had taken the first four dances of his beloved. That she had instigated the commitments was ignored by the infatuated man.

"Oh, I'm sorry, I am already engaged for those dances," Lydia said with a shy smile. "Lord Warburton has just introduced me to Sir Ralph Anderton; he is a very interesting man. He insisted he have those dances and then escort me into supper; I was quite overawed at his manner."

"The next two then?" Percy almost ground out.

"Of course, my dear Mr West; my night would not be complete without a dance with yourself," Lydia placed her hand on Percy's arm, which for such a small action, went a long way to mollify him.

Eleanor rolled her eyes. She had never noticed Lydia was so overt in her flirting, or was it that Eleanor was jealous of her friend's success? She hoped not, but she was not convinced her unkind feelings were there purely as a result of Lydia's behaviour. She had felt a pang of jealousy when Lydia had so easily secured Mr Heaton for the first two. Her feelings went deeper than mere jealousy though, for the first time since they met, Eleanor felt being with Lydia was not necessarily a good idea. Their opinions on acceptable behaviour differed enormously.

When the party was led into the ballroom and the music began, Eleanor took her place in the set with Archie. He was a pleasant gentleman whom she liked.

"How long do you stay in Bath?" Eleanor asked as they danced.

"We have no definite plans; it all depends on Joseph really," Archie said pleasantly, trying not to watch Lydia dancing a short way further up the set with Joseph.

"Oh? Has he something particular in mind?" Eleanor asked, curiously.

Archie looked a little uncomfortable. "Well, he's usually the one who has all the ideas: Percy and myself just follow most of the time; we prefer it that way."

"You or Mr Heaton would prefer it?" Eleanor asked with a raise of an eyebrow.

Archie laughed despite his moment of panic at revealing too much of his friendships. "I suppose it could be a little of both," he admitted.

"You all seem very good friends," Eleanor continued. She wanted to find out more about Joseph, but it would be inappropriate to openly pry.

"We've known each other for years," Archie admitted. "Since we were in leading strings; we went to school together and, although we were an unlikely trio, we've stuck together even when branching out."

"It must be nice to have long-lasting friendships."

"Isn't it just?" Archie seized the opportunity he had been waiting for. "How long have you and Lady Lydia been friends?"

"Only a year. We also met at school," Eleanor said.

"I'm surprised you are not gracing the balls in London; I'm sure Lady Lydia would be a hit. I can never imagine her being one of the wallflowers sitting out a dance." Archie said without thinking about his words, as many young women, including Eleanor sat out at balls.

Eleanor suppressed a smile. "She would certainly be a hit in London, but I'm sure the society of Bath is appreciative of her presence."

"Oh, I'll say we are!" Archie said with feeling. "I was never as happy as when we were introduced. Without her, the society would be tedious. When I am doing anything other than speaking to her, I am counting the moments until I am returned to her company. She makes me delighted with everything."

Eleanor presumed Archie did not realise that his friend had already declared himself to Lydia. "I'm sure she is equally as happy," she said diplomatically.

The two dances ended to Eleanor's relief. Mr Brinklow was a pleasant man, but an hour spent talking of Lydia was tedious even of her best friend. Eleanor was led to Joseph by Mr Brinklow. She smiled at Joseph, but he detected a slight note of strain in her smile. He looked quizzically at Archie, but the young man looked perfectly happy, especially as he was escorting Lydia into the set. Joseph offered his arm to Eleanor and joined the set a little away from Archie and Lydia.

The dancing started, and at first Joseph watched Eleanor. She was quite tall; she came to his shoulder, but she moved lightly. She would never be the petite Miss Lady Lydia was, but she seemed in proportion somehow. He liked that she seemed smaller than him, but he did not have to stoop whilst dancing with her.

He smiled at one of their turns and opened the conversation. "The colour of your dress brings out the green in your eyes," he said, a great compliment from one usually quite reticent in giving genuine compliments.

"Thank you," Eleanor responded, a little surprised he had noticed her eye colour.

"A little quiet tonight, Miss Johnson; are you not in the mood for entertainments?" Joseph continued. He had expected more from his words, she was usually so quick to tease and ridicule him; when it was not forthcoming, he missed it. He realised he should not always expect a young lady to swoon at his compliments, but for a strange reason he did want Eleanor to be affected by them. Much to his chagrin it was clear she had hardly registered that he had praised her.

Eleanor smiled. "I'm always in the mood for dancing, Mr Heaton, but sometimes I allow myself to become diverted, my apologies."

"There is no need to apologise; I'm just trying to solve the puzzle as to what my friend could have said that would put you out of mood with the rest of us," Joseph said. The quick look and blush to Eleanor's cheeks convinced him he was correct. "Come," he said gently. "What has the buffoon said to upset you?"

Eleanor groaned; she should have been more circumspect. "I'm ashamed to admit he has insulted only my vanity, so he has done nothing wrong, as it is my own fault for being too sensitive," she replied sounding light-hearted.

Joseph bristled, something that surprised him, but he pushed his own feelings aside; he would kill Archie later. "I cannot image you are a naturally vain person; you seem far too sensible for that, but if you don't tell me I shall have to walk across and call out Archie for insulting my delightful dance partner," Joseph said with a smile, but Eleanor would never realise just how serious his words were.

"A dance spent complimenting my friend should not upset me. See? I told you it was my vanity at fault. You can excuse Mr Brinklow and, in fact, if you wish to tell me how wonderful my friend is, which she is, I promise not to be offended at all!" Eleanor said, hoping she put enough lightness in her words to hide how much the incident had stung.

Joseph groaned. "It is worse than I thought; I am definitely going to have to call him out now."

"Are you declaring yourself my protector, Mr Heaton?" Eleanor said teasingly.

"I certainly am," Joseph said with conviction. "I can think of no one else I would rather protect."

Eleanor laughed, a genuine laugh, her hurt forgotten. "I would be honoured, but I hope you are a good shot, or I shan't be protected for long."

"I am an excellent shot, but Archie would beat me with a sword, so I shall have to insist on pistols," Joseph said in all seriousness.

"In that case, I shall relax; you will emerge the victor, and I shall still have my protector. It sounds like a fine day's work," Eleanor responded.

"To make up for the buffoon who goes by the name of Archie, could I persuade yourself and Lady Lydia to accompany us to the theatre tomorrow evening? I have a box booked, and Mr West's aunt will be joining us, so it is perfectly respectable. I would be delighted if you would agree," Joseph persuaded.

"I shall ask Lady Moore and Lady Lydia," Eleanor replied. She was not sure how Lydia would respond to being in their company again so soon. They would be in danger of openly being the favourites to any onlookers wondering if Lydia would make a match with any of them. The fact Eleanor wanted to would ensure she would do her best to persuade Lydia to accept the invitation.

"Perfect," Joseph said.

*

Archie and Percy left the ball a few minutes ahead of Joseph, but he soon caught them up. When he did he grabbed Archie by the shoulder and swung him round to face him. A punch caught Archie on the side of his jaw and sent him reeling before the young man realised what had happened.

"What the hell has got into you, Joe?" Archie demanded, sitting on the pavement, holding his jaw. Percy had put himself between Archie and Joseph, not quite sure why such an outburst had happened. "Are you in your cups?"

"That's for insulting a young woman who would make ten of you," Joseph snarled. He had been boiling with anger all night, but had managed to keep it in check until now.

"I was a perfect gentleman to Lady Lydia," Archie snapped, standing and brushing down his breeches.

"You're so wrapped up in that chit you haven't even realised you offended her best friend have you?" Joseph said with disgust.

"Miss Johnson? Why, I never said anything to upset her!" Archie said defensively.

"Are you sure about that?" Joseph snapped, wanting to shake his friend. "Think over your conversation."

Archie stood and thought back over what he had said. "We talked about Lady Lydia. I just said society would be tedious without her, and she would never sit out a dance." Archie was convinced there was nothing wrong with what he had mentioned.

"Oh, Archie," Percy said with a groan, realising immediately what a fool his friend had been.

"Have you noticed anything at the dances we have already attended?" Joseph asked but continued before his friend could respond. "The number of men to women is vastly different. Ladies sit out at dances, Miss Johnson has sat out at both dances we attended. How the devil do you think it made her feel to have the fact she did not dance every dance commented on and Lady Lydia did? You buffoon!"

"I didn't think," Archie said quietly.

"No, you certainly didn't," Joseph said.

"She is only the plain friend though; I suppose you were right: I haven't been making a fuss of her like you instructed," Archie said in his defence. Almost before the words left his mouth, he was grabbed by the cravat and hauled against the wall.

"If you ever insult Miss Johnson in such a way again, I will give you such a beating, you will wish we had never met!" Joseph snarled, his face only inches from Archie's face.

Archie gulped; the expression on Joseph's face was pure murder. He had never seen him respond to anything so violently before; he was more likely to laugh or ridicule but never resort to violence.

Archie held up his hands. "I'm sorry; I was being unfair. I will apologise."

"You will leave it," Joseph said. "I don't want you making an even bigger hash of it." He let go of his friend. "I have invited Miss Johnson and Lady Lydia to the theatre tomorrow evening as an apology. You," he said, still glaring at Archie. "Say anything wrong, and I will personally throw you into the stalls."

"But Joseph, you will never get a box at this late stage. Bath is full; all the boxes will be already booked," Percy said.

"Leave it to me; we will have a box tomorrow evening," Joseph said before turning and walking in the direction of Queens Square.

Chapter 5

Lydia was excited about the trip to the theatre and readily accepted the invitation that was received at Henrietta Street early the following morning.

"Sir Ralph is going to the same show; he spoke about it last night. He wanted to invite me, but unfortunately his box is full; at least this way he shall see I am not reliant on him for my entertainment," Lydia gushed as the pair breakfasted.

"Do you like Sir Ralph?" Eleanor asked. He had seemed quite boorish from the few moments they had conversed. He was also a lot older than Lydia.

"He was very attentive," Lydia said with a slight wave of her hand, as if being attentive to her was expected. "He has also two properties to speak of and a title."

"I would hope liking or loving someone would be more important than how many properties a person has," Eleanor said.

"Oh, my dear!" Lydia exclaimed with a laugh. "You may be older than me by two months, but I am older in experience! One has to assess which beaux would provide the most; I have standards of living I wish to be maintained when I marry, or even better, improved."

"I feel like a rustic next to you; I was hoping for love," Eleanor said with a shrug.

"And maybe we shall find it, but we need to make sure he is rich and titled into the bargain," Lydia said laughing.

"Mr West hasn't got a title," Eleanor pointed out. She felt sorry for Percy; he seemed harmless enough and totally besotted by Lydia; it was not fair to him if she was only using him.

"I know; I've been mulling over that problem since he declared his affection for me. It is a worry; he has no future prospects," Lydia said dismissively. "He is nice enough, but unless he inherits from some distant uncle, I cannot see my attachment being long-lasting. I have to consider my future."

"Why not tell him that then?" Eleanor would always prefer honesty even if it was not pleasant.

"Because, my dear friend, he is young, attractive and will make my other beaux jealous, thus encouraging them to try even harder," Lydia explained as if she were talking to a small child.

"I'm suddenly glad I am not as popular as you," Eleanor said with feeling.

*

Two sedan chairs were engaged to take the young ladies to the theatre. The journey was only a few minutes' walk from Henrietta Street, but Lady Moore would not hear of them walking through the streets of Bath during the evening.

The short journey was taken at a rapid pace, the chair bearers welcoming the light weight of their occupants. Bath housed quite a few elderly ladies and gentlemen who could barely fit into the chairs, which made carrying them a trial. There were rules as to what the bearers could charge, depending on how far the journey, but most bearers thought weight should have also been taken into consideration.

Eleanor and Lydia joined the throng entering the building. They were relieved of their pelisses and bonnets and smoothed down their dresses. Lydia had on a stylish cream gown, which had layers of ruffles across the hem. Eleanor had chosen a champagne coloured taffeta that warmed her skin tone.

They were soon joined by the three gentlemen and Mr West's aunt and older cousin. Both were dominating Percy and taking his time, much to his annoyance, as it left Archie free rein to monopolise Lydia. Archie offered his arm to Lydia, but not before he made his bow to Eleanor and told her how spectacular she looked. Lydia took Archie's arm and moved into the theatre. Joseph had been holding back a little but moved forward with a smile on his face, which Eleanor returned.

"What mischief have you been up to, Mr Heaton?" Eleanor asked, referring to the change in Archie's behaviour.

Joseph looked back at her with an expression of mock hurt. "I am wounded you would think I interfered in any way." The punch he had lashed out with had been given specifically so the bruise could be well hidden by collar and cravat. Joseph did not wish Eleanor be made to feel worse by his interference.

"You expect me to believe you?" Eleanor asked, raising an eyebrow.

"I do expect you to believe me and, for your information, you do look stunning," Joseph said. It was true; although she was no great beauty, with her eyes sparkling at him, her cheeks lightly blushing and a smile dancing around her lips, she was very attractive. He wondered that he had not noticed it before or perhaps he had, and that was why he enjoyed watching her so much.

"When you grow up being introduced as the intelligent one, you know stunning is a word that should not be associated with oneself," Eleanor said honestly. She was not offended by the false praise; she knew Joseph liked her, and that was enough. Well, maybe not enough, but the best she could hope for.

"You never mentioned that all your family were blind," Joseph responded, and they entered the box with Eleanor laughing at his words.

The party was seated to the approval of three of the seven occupants of the box. Lydia was seated at the front with Archie while Percy, his aunt and cousin sat closely behind them. Joseph sat himself and Eleanor a little away from the others. He did not wish to hear Percy's mutterings but wanted to be free to enjoy Eleanor's company. So, Archie, Joseph and Eleanor thought the box was ideally set; Lydia did not care with whom she sat as long as they gave her enough attention, and Percy was left to be the reluctant companion to two older relatives. He was doubly grieved because it had been Joseph who had invited them so, by rights, he should have been the one to entertain them.

The play commenced and, although not the best any of the party had seen, it was acceptable. It was a comedy that created enough laughs so those who wanted a private conversation could have it in the noise the other theatre-goers created. Archie was able to whisper sweet nothings into Lydia's ear, which was noticed by Joseph.

"My friend seems to be smitten with Lady Lydia," he whispered to Eleanor, his lips close to her ear.

"Both your friends are, I fear," Eleanor whispered in return, not adding she hoped he was not, but she accepted that it was inevitable.

"It looks like she will have a difficult choice, if she is serious about either of them," Joseph responded. From her actions, he could not guess which one Lydia preferred.

"I'm finding Lydia does not share the same ideals as I," Eleanor said obtusely.

"Oh? How's that?" Joseph asked, immediately curious.

Eleanor did not wish to go into too much detail; she did not wish to cause trouble between Lydia and her beaux, but she felt comfortable with Joseph and wanted to express some of her frustration and confusion. She normally would have confided in one of her sisters but needed someone who knew Lydia to truly understand what troubled her.

"She sees marriage more as a business transaction than a joining of two well matched people," Eleanor responded after a moment's thought.

Joseph could see the difficulty Eleanor was having by the expression on her face, but he wanted to encourage more from her. "A lot of people see it as a transaction."

"I know; my own father does: he wanted all four girls to marry titles, the higher the better," Eleanor acknowledged. "I just did not expect to hear the same calculating sentiment from a young woman, I suppose."

Joseph had been given two very interesting pieces of information. He wanted to find out more. "So, you have to marry a title?" he asked.

Eleanor sighed, "Maybe, but maybe not; it's complicated."

Joseph's insides lurched at the sound of the sigh; it was so heartfelt and sad, something that he would not have associated with Eleanor; she always seemed so playful. On instinct more than any conscious thought, he reached out and took hold of her hand.

Eleanor took a sharp breath; they were both wearing gloves, but it felt so wonderful to feel a strong hand around hers. For the first time in her life, she felt smaller than she actually was, and it made her heart race. She looked at Joseph questioningly and then looked pointedly at the other occupants in the box. If the gesture were noticed, there would be questions to answer.

Joseph smiled in reassurance; they were in a darkened box at the rear out of the light. If anyone turned towards them, he could release her hand quickly, but for now he was more than happy holding it. His finger could feel her pulse, and he felt warmth spreading through him knowing hers was beating rapidly.

"Tell me why it is complicated," he encouraged quietly.

Eleanor leaned slightly towards him; she did not wish for her whispers to be overheard or to disturb the others, but it did make her pulse increase further to be so close to the man who filled her every thought.

"My father arranged the marriage between Rosalind and the Duke of Sudworth, as I've already mentioned," Eleanor started. "The aim was for us all to marry gentlemen with titles. We come with large dowries, but for some reason my father wishes for us all to have grand titles. Obviously none of us agreed with it."

"Why not? It's not unusual to want to marry a title; you've said Lady Lydia does even though she plays with the affections of my two friends. I don't think they have realised quite yet they don't rank high enough for her," Joseph said.

Eleanor inwardly groaned; he did not sound annoyed but, if he told his friends of her foolish words, her stay in Bath would become a lot more uncomfortable. She should have been more circumspect, but she hoped her instinct was right and she could trust him. "I am from a society that has no titles, so to myself and my sisters, it is irrelevant what title the man has we are to marry. I'm afraid, for us, it was an idea from a fickle man that has caused no end of problems, because he has now thrown something even more complicated into the mix." She did not want to explain that, if either herself or Grace, the two remaining unmarried sisters, did not find suitable titles, they would be forced to marry the man whom their father had chosen to continue running his businesses.

"You are right; it does sound complicated," Joseph replied. He was slightly reassured about her denial at wanting a title; she sounded convincing and had not appeared to long for such.

"I know; sometimes I wonder that any of us have grown up sensible with the parents we have. Perhaps it had more to do with the good character of our nanny than anything else," Eleanor said with feeling.

"Most people are grateful when they have the care of a good nanny; they do seem to make up for numerous mistakes by parents," Joseph responded. "So how can we tempt you to accompany us on another excursion after this evening?" he asked. For some reason he needed to know he would see her again soon. They might see one another each morning in the Pump Rooms, but that was not enough; he wanted to make firm plans.

Eleanor flushed with pleasure; she had to keep reminding herself he was a sociable person, and it was not a particular request to see herself. "What had you in mind?" she asked.

"I do wish to take you on that phaeton ride we did not go on a few days ago, but I think it would be pleasant if we met at the Lower Assembly Rooms tomorrow evening. Could I secure the first two with you?" he asked with a smile.

"Lydia has mentioned we will be attending, so I would be delighted to accept your offer of dances, thank you," Eleanor replied.

"Excellent," Joseph said, squeezing her hand before reluctantly letting go. There was no point risking being caught, even if the chances were remote.

They all stood, enjoying refreshments that had been delivered shortly before the end of the act. At the interval, a knock struck the box door. Sir Ralph was shown into the box, and Lydia left Archie's side.

"Sir Ralph, what a lovely surprise; I had not seen you in the crowd," Lydia lied. She had seen him as soon as she had been seated and had turned her profile to its best effect accordingly.

"I have hardly seen the play, I could not stop looking at such a beauty!" Sir Ralph said, his portly figure quivering with feeling.

"Oh, you are such a sweetheart!" Lydia responded, unaware of the look Joseph was sending to his friends. Eleanor saw it and blushed for her friend; it was clear Joseph was trying to raise their awareness to Lydia being the fickle woman she was.

"Bless my soul, if I'd known you were a lover of the theatre, I would hire a box every week and beg you to join me," Sir Ralph continued.

"I would always be happy to accept an invitation to the theatre," Lydia said, her eyes shining up at the gentleman.

"You'd have a hell of a job securing a box; they're booked up for weeks in advance," Archie interposed, unable to resist trying to ridicule Sir Ralph's attempts at gaining Lady Lydia's affections.

Eleanor frowned slightly; if what Archie said was correct, she wondered how Joseph had managed to secure a box, he was so recent to Bath. Her attention returned to Sir Ralph; she had to give him credit: he was continuing as if the rest of the party did not exist; that took some belief in oneself in her opinion.

"My dear Lady Lydia, please tell me you are attending the ball at the Assembly Rooms tomorrow? I beg you to allow me to dance the first two with you and take you into supper."

Lydia fluttered her fan as if contemplating her options before smiling and inclining her head slightly. "I would be delighted," she said quietly.

"I shall return to the stalls filled with anticipation for tomorrow, my dear child," Sir Ralph said and left the box.

There was a moment's quiet once the older gentleman left before Percy burst out, "Lydia, I thought you'd allow me to have the first two with you tomorrow!"

Lydia looked at him with an expression of sorrow. "My dear Mr West, you never asked; how was I to know you wished to dance with me? It would have been very arrogant of me to presume, would it not?"

Percy was all forgiveness because, of course, Lydia would not have presumed; it was his own fault, and he secured the next two dances before the party resumed their seating in time for the second act.

Joseph inclined his head towards Eleanor to whisper in her ear. "I think the best actress tonight is not on the stage," he said seriously.

Eleanor was tempted to laugh at the comment, but she kept control of herself. She did not reply even though Lydia had behaved appallingly towards the two gentlemen; to do so would be a betrayal of her friendship, but she did tap Joseph's arm with her fan in punishment. It was enough to make him chuckle, a sound that would fill her dreams for many days.

Chapter 6

Before they departed for the Lower Assembly Rooms the following evening, Eleanor entered Lydia's bedchamber. Lydia dismissed her maid when Eleanor sat on Lydia's bed. When the maid had gone, Lydia looked at her friend in the mirror with a smile. "I hope to have two more proposals by the end of the evening," she said confidently.

"Two? You expect both Mr Brinklow and Sir Ralph to offer for you?" Eleanor asked in surprise. "Would they not speak to your father first?"

"Not at all. I have dropped enough hints that I would frown at such behaviour," Lydia said with conviction.

"But that is the normal tradition, isn't it?" Eleanor asked, thinking that Lydia was playing a dangerous game.

"Yes, but I want to know exactly what my options are before my father knows. He will only try to interfere, and I want to decide who to marry before he decides for me."

Eleanor understood that sentiment and softened towards her friend. "I knew you were interested in love deep down."

"Love? Oh, Eleanor, you can be silly sometimes! I want to know the man's prospects before I decide, not whether or not I love him. He will love me; that will have to be enough for both of us," Lydia responded, patting her hair with approval before standing. "It's a pity there isn't more of a choice, but unfortunately Bath seems to be a little sparse of suitable gentlemen at the moment and, from what Papa has said, we won't be returning to London this season or next. I am not foolish enough to wait another two years."

Eleanor shook her head and followed Lydia downstairs. Her friend was obviously the daughter her own father should have had. They would find they had a lot in common if they ever met. Lydia chatted throughout the carriage journey to the Assembly Rooms, oblivious to the widening gap between herself and her friend.

The Assembly Rooms did not seem as crowded as they usually were. They found out a large ball was being given in Wells. Lydia was most put out they had not received an invitation, but she was mollified a little with the arrival of her beaux, who surrounded her, offering ever more excessive compliments than each other.

"You see before you a glut of fools," came the deep rumble that Eleanor welcomed so much.

Eleanor turned to face Joseph with a smile. "What? You aren't going to tell me my eyes sparkle more than all the chandeliers in the room or that my hair is purer than spun gold? I'm so disappointed," she sighed, her eyes sparkling with laughter.

"I would prefer to speak the truth and say to you the knowledge that you are waiting to dance with me will always ensure I wait with anticipation of the musicians starting," Joseph said. He was smiling, but his eyes looked a shade darker than normal; they took Eleanor's breath away.

Luckily for Eleanor the musicians chose that moment to strum their instruments, and Eleanor was led onto the dance floor, her heart beating far more than it had been a few moments previously.

As they danced Joseph began to tease. "I must point out you are dimming the light from the chandeliers; I must ask you to stop sparkling or no one else will be able to see."

"I find I cannot help it, Mr Heaton; I am just so naturally sparkly," Eleanor responded in kind.

"I am surely dancing with a diamond," Joseph continued. "If I don't watch out I shall have Sir Ralph asking to take you into supper."

"And I, of course, will accept, because he is a 'Sir' and one must encourage a title," Eleanor said with mock seriousness.

"Of course, I understand completely, and I can only apologise for being so lacking."

"I shall forgive you, as you are a passably decent dancer," Eleanor responded. She had never danced with anyone who suited her more, so the words created a mischievous grin.

Joseph groaned inwardly. He had not thought his partner could draw him in further, but the expression on her face had just done it. He could not remember the last time he had met someone who entertained him or beguiled him more. He was shocked with the realisation he was rapidly becoming smitten with Miss Johnson.

They danced the two dances and then Eleanor was engaged with Archie, still eager to make amends for his lack of manners. After one dance with Sir Ralph, who just used it to get as much information about Lydia as he could, she danced with Percy.

Eleanor accepted a drink from Percy before he left her to seek out Lydia. Eleanor smiled to herself; it was really becoming a battle of wills between the three gentlemen. She left the ball room and stepped out onto the balcony overlooking the gardens of the Lower Assembly Rooms. It was pleasant to attend a ball with fewer people; there was room to move, and she did not feel as constrained as she sometimes did.

She spotted Joseph standing on the edge of the balcony, smoking a cigarillo, looking out over the moonlit gardens. He was a fine man, tall and broad, filling his dark frock coat. She wondered if she would ever meet a man who was as perfect as he was, and the thought saddened her a little. He had so much, but she could never compete with the type of women he would be attracted to. She had seen it often enough: good looks attracted good looks; it was the way of the world.

Joseph turned; he knew she was there. It was because of the prickling on the back of his neck that occurred whenever she was near. He smiled at her before crossing the space between them. "You've escaped as well?" he asked, his voice low. There were people in the gardens, but it was not the done thing to be outside alone with a person of the opposite gender.

"Only for a moment; I have more dances promised, I'll have you know," Eleanor said with a smile.

"Lucky blighters! If the convention were different, I would be dancing with you again," Joseph said truthfully. It was the only time he was allowed to touch her, and the urge did not go away after an hour of dancing.

"Oh," Eleanor said, a little lost for words. "I thought you would have a line of people begging you to dance."

"Even if I did, I would not wish to dance with them as much as I do you," Joseph said, moving a little closer. Her eyes had opened wider in surprise at his compliments, and he found them to be acting like a magnet to him, pulling him towards her.

"Thank you for the praise; I shall treasure it," Eleanor said with a smile and a nervous sip of her drink.

"I want some wine," Joseph said quietly.

"Oh, shall we return inside?" Eleanor asked, moving towards the French door.

"No, I want to taste wine this way," Joseph said before pulling her towards him. He had thrown his cigarillo to burn out on the stone terrace before wrapping his arms around Eleanor's waist and gently putting his lips on hers.

Eleanor's arms flailed to the side for a moment before she wrapped them around Joseph's neck, taking care not to spill the little wine that was left in the glass. His kiss sent a frisson of pleasure through her that stopped all coherent thought.

Joseph was aware he was taking a risk, but he had wanted to kiss her for days; he just had not realised it until that moment. He teased her lips, making her eyes flutter open and close again as he increased the pressure. She tasted of wine and mixed with the taste of the cigarillo was perfect. She was tall enough to come slightly higher than his shoulder. Seeming to fit against him perfectly, the thought he had found a perfect match flitted through his mind before her kisses removed all thoughts.

Eleanor mirrored Joseph's every move until she became a little more confident. She pulled away slightly and bit his lower lip gently, which resulted in a heartfelt groan and a crush against him. She did not wish any of it to stop, but she knew it had to. She reluctantly pulled away from him and leant against the wall, trying to catch her breath.

Joseph stepped back a little for respectability's sake, but it was reassured to notice Eleanor's deep breathing matched his own.

"I think I need to drink more wine," he said finally, smiling at her.

Eleanor laughed, "I never realised it could be such a pleasant pastime."

Joseph grinned in appreciation. "One better shared, I think."

"Yes," Eleanor said; taking a sip of her wine, she hoped it would help to calm her, but her heart rate increased when she saw the look in Joseph's eyes. "We mustn't," she said quietly. She wanted to, goodness she wanted to, but she was not fool enough to risk being found in such a position.

"We will kiss again," Joseph responded, reaching out and cupping her cheek before letting go. "We are definitely going to be doing that again."

Joseph walked away and left Eleanor to calm down. It was not appropriate they should enter the room together, but the terrace seemed a little darker without his presence. She left the terrace to enter through the door from which she had found her escape. Now it felt as if it had led her into another world; her whole outlook had changed.

For the remainder of the evening it was as if Eleanor was present but not completely. Her mind was full of feelings she had experienced for the first time. She had no idea what his intentions were, but for now that did not concern her; when you had been kissed so thoroughly, it was difficult to think beyond that.

She did not see Joseph until the end of the evening. She blushed when he approached and was reassured when he smiled at her, his eyes warming and sending even more sensation to her tumultuous stomach.

"I suggest we take a trip out tomorrow, if Lady Lydia agrees," Joseph started. "She has seen the delights of Bradford-on-Avon but has not yet seen the treasures that Wells has to offer."

"No, I have not," Lydia replied, interrupting the conversation. "I would have seen some of it tonight, if I'd received an invitation to the Blake's ball, but a Lady is obviously not good enough to secure an invite."

Eleanor cringed at the petulant tone Lydia used; she was impressed when Joseph smiled down at Lady Lydia. "We would have missed your company if you had accepted an invitation. I can only be grateful you did not. Please let us take phaetons out for the day tomorrow."

Lydia had smiled sweetly at Joseph's words. She was mollified for the moment. "Of course, we would be delighted to accompany you; it will be our little adventure."

"Splendid," Joseph responded with every intention that his phaeton would race ahead with himself and Eleanor on board, so he could enjoy some more of those kisses.

*

Lydia walked into Eleanor's bedchamber. She did not knock, always confident of a warm welcome. Eleanor was in bed, reading. She was trying to concentrate on anything else in the hope she would be able to sleep instead of replaying over and over again the kisses she had experienced.

Lydia sat on the edge of Eleanor's bed. "You doubted me, didn't you?" Lydia asked smugly.

"I don't think so; to what do you refer?" Eleanor responded.

"They both wish to marry me!" Lydia replied triumphantly.

"Mr Brinklow and Sir Ralph?" Eleanor asked astounded. Her feeling was not astonishment that Lydia had been asked, but that she had persuaded three men to be open with her rather than gaining the approval of Lord Moore first.

"Of course! Now all I need is a proposal from Mr Heaton, and then I shall make my decision," Lydia said leaning back against the post with a sigh. "If only they all had titles I would be happier, and it would make it an easier decision."

"Mr-Mr Heaton?" Eleanor stuttered; she felt the colour drain from her face, but Lydia was too wrapped up in her own concerns to notice.

"Oh, yes, he has been more reserved than Mr Brinklow and Mr West, but I see the way he watches me; a little encouragement and he will be mine," Lydia said confidently. "I need to work quickly with him because Mr West is becoming impatient, the poor lamb."

"Are you going to accept Mr West?" Eleanor asked hopefully.

"I have no idea," Lydia laughed. "Sir Ralph is older and not as attractive as the others, but he is titled and has money, although not as much as I would hope."

"You know how much they are all worth?" Eleanor was astounded at her friend. She appeared so carefree and yet underneath, it was clear she was totally focused on her scheme.

"Of course! Well, actually our three friends have only hinted at their income being around the thousand a year mark," Lydia said with derision. "I would not consider that amount normally, but with there being no opportunity of having a season in London, I am forced to."

"And Sir Ralph?"

"A healthier two thousand a year," Lydia said, pulling a face. "If only he were younger and thinner, my decision would be made all the easier."

"You would not marry someone you did not like?" Eleanor asked. "What about being with him?" she tried to be diplomatic, but the thought of not marrying someone she was attracted to filled her with fear.

"Oh, that, once I have provided an heir, I shall encourage him to seek a mistress," Lydia said airily. "It's what most women do."

Eleanor shook her head in wonder. "I would hate to be in such a marriage."

"Oh, I shall have lovers," Lydia said with a smile as if she were reassuring Eleanor, rather than increasing the young woman's horror.

"Of course," Eleanor replied, dumbfounded.

"Hopefully this way, I shall be still in contact with our three friends if I do decide to marry Sir Ralph."

"You sound as if you have already decided," Eleanor said dully.

"I have, I suppose; I just need to find out Mr Heaton's prospects. He's the one makes me the most curious; he is difficult to read, more of a challenge."

"Oh."

"I shall enjoy conquering him the most," Lydia said standing. "I am off to bed; I need to look my best in the morning: I have hearts to conquer!" With a laugh, she left the room, leaving Eleanor to flop back on her pillows. What had seemed like the perfect evening had just turned into a nightmare. Of course, Joseph would fall for Lydia; they were both by far the most handsome people in Bath.

Eleanor rolled onto her stomach with a groan; it was going to be a long night.

Chapter 7

Eleanor had recovered her equilibrium by morning. She was being foolish; Lydia had no idea what had passed between Eleanor and Joseph: she was just treating him as she had her other conquests. If she knew what had passed between the pair, Eleanor was convinced Lydia would cease to try and ensnare him. She hoped.

If she was being honest with herself, Eleanor was not sure what had happened between herself and Joseph. It had been delightful, of that there was no doubt; and he had said it was going to happen again, but he had not mentioned anything about courtship, so perhaps Eleanor was reading too much into the kisses.

She readied herself with extra care, donning a deep green pelisse that was decorated with gold braiding. Her hat was of matching green material with a gold organza ribbon falling down her back. Short gold gloves and reticule finished the outfit off to best effect.

She joined Lydia in the drawing room. Lydia had chosen a deep blue pelisse with white decoration, topped by a white and blue bonnet. The bonnet was tilted at a jaunty angle, emphasising the petite face beneath it.

They were collected by two phaetons and Mr West on horseback. The whole party were surprised when Lydia hopped into Mr Heaton's phaeton without help and announced she was going to ride with him.

Joseph and Eleanor's eyes met briefly; Joseph looking apologetic with a half-smile on his lips. This was certainly not how he had planned his day. Eleanor looked resigned, which alerted him to what Lydia was planning; he was determined they would all stay together as a group. He wanted no part in any scheme of Lydia's.

The party started off, Archie careful he did not talk too much of Lydia to the detriment of his passenger. He was uncharacteristically annoyed though; he had an idea of what Joseph planned to do: he should have known Joseph would win in the battle that was Lady Lydia and, for the first time since they had met, he despised his friend.

The conversation between Eleanor and himself was polite and irregular. Both were watching what was passing between the pair in the other phaeton, each tied up in their own doubts. Percy kept close to Lydia, but it was obvious most of Lydia's attention was focused on Joseph. When for the tenth time in as many minutes Lydia threw her head back in laughter, Archie could keep politeness going no longer.

"I shouldn't be surprised the gutter-rat is gaining more ground than anyone else; of course, it was planned before we even arrived here!" Archie ground out.

Eleanor was surprised at the tone of voice and turned to Archie. "I don't understand you, Mr Brinklow; are you saying Mr Heaton had some plan he has been carrying out?"

Archie stilled; he should say no more, but an ill-timed touch of Lydia's arm by Joseph sent him into a blinding anger. "It would cause offence to you if I told you, which I do not wish to do," he said between gritted teeth. He was sorely tempted to ram into the back of the phaeton and overturn them all.

An ominous feeling settled inside Eleanor, but she needed to know what Archie was referring to. "Mr Brinklow, please tell me the truth. You are clearly aware of something about the people I am associating with, and I would like to know what it is. I do not like the feeling of being part of some grand scheme." Her voice was steady, but she felt nothing other than dread inside.

Archie looked at Eleanor, and all he could see was a stern expression. He presumed she was as angry as he felt, and he decided he had found an ally in her. "It saddens me to say this but, before we ventured into Bath, we knew of Lady Lydia's presence; Percy wrote of her in great detail."

This came as no surprise to Eleanor, so she nodded in encouragement.

"Joseph gave us some advice; he said to befriend and make a fuss of the plain friend, and it would go a long way in securing the affections of the one you really wished to secure. Do not take from my words that any of us considers you plain, Miss Johnson; I am merely repeating the words of a cad," Archie said.

"Don't trouble yourself," Eleanor reassured him. "I am under no illusion of my limitations." She felt sick to her stomach.

"We actually thought he wasn't showing Lady Lydia any preference, and last night I specifically asked him to allow me to take Lady Lydia in my equipage, to which he agreed. I was foolish enough to tell him of my feelings for her. I thought he was being supportive yet, the moment we reach your address, Lady Lydia is in his phaeton and not mine," Archie said bitterly.

Eleanor swallowed, trying to keep control when all she wanted to do was sit down and cry. Of course, he had been playing with her; in her heart she had known he was too good for her. He was handsome, intelligent and popular; why would he look at someone as ordinary as herself? She had been holding onto a dream that was not real, could never be real, and yet she was reeling from the hurt when the reality of the situation was pointed out to her.

The laughter continued from the phaeton in front and, after a few minutes, Eleanor decided she could stand no more. "Mr Brinklow, I'm afraid I have a terrible headache developing. I know it must grieve you to leave the party, but I wonder would it be possible for you to return me to Henrietta Street?"

Archie was immediately aware it must have been his words that upset her and tried to make amends. "I apologise, Miss Johnson; my words have hurt you, and I honestly did not wish it."

"Your words have only proved what a fool we have both been in believing the words of a scoundrel, but that doesn't prevent the headache developing at a steady pace. Please could you put me down if you cannot return me?" The urge to leave the group was great.

"I shall return you this instant," Archie said. He shouted to the others and, when they paused, he caught them up. "Miss Johnson is unwell. I am returning her home."

Eleanor did not meet Joseph's eyes, so she failed to see the look of concern in them. Lydia wished Eleanor well, but did not make any attempt to turn back herself. Joseph whispered to her, but Lydia dismissed his words. "Of course, we should continue; Eleanor would not wish us to spoil our plans, would you Eleanor?"

"Oh no," Eleanor replied. "All of your plans have been so long in the making, I would not wish for them to alter at this stage."

Joseph frowned at her words and looked at Archie, but he was also not meeting Joseph's gaze. Percy interjected before the party separated. "We only made these plans last night Miss Johnson; we can return with you."

Eleanor smiled a genuine smile. "Thank you, Mr West, but I shall be perfectly fine with Mr Brinklow's company. I hope you have an enjoyable outing."

The phaeton turned, and the three who were left behind watched it disappear. Joseph's frown was deep, something was seriously wrong; as well as not meeting his gaze, Eleanor had been as pale as a sheet. He cursed his idea for the outing, but politeness forced him to continue. It was going to be a long day.

*

Eleanor crumpled onto her bed and let the tears fall. She had been used and had never suspected for an instant. If she was the intelligent one in the family, God help the others. She cried for half an hour and then forced herself to dry her eyes.

She could not stay with Lydia. If she returned saying Joseph had offered for her, Eleanor was sure for the first time in her life she would have a hysterical fit. No, she had to get away.

She paced her bedchamber while deciding what to do. When she formulated a plan, she sought out Lady Moore. Her pale complexion and red eyes would give credence to her lies.

Eleanor convinced Lady Moore a family catastrophe was forcing her to leave suddenly, and time was of the essence. A footman was sent to obtain a ticket for her on the stagecoach, and a maid quickly packed her belongings. Luckily for Eleanor she was a resourceful young woman and did not lack in either money or ability to take herself half way across country.

She told Lady Moore she was returning home but, when the stage arrived in Bristol, she changed her ticket to one taking her to Rosalind's town in the North. There was no benefit to going to her parents; they would immediately want to know all the details as to why she was returning home, and she had been warned by a letter from Annabelle not to return home, because Mr Wadeson could assess her to make his decision as to which sister he would marry.

Rosalind had insisted she wanted all of her sisters to spend time with her before they wed; she was hopeful of arranging marriages to suitable men, so Eleanor was quite justified in travelling to her sister's home, but Eleanor just wanted the comfort her sister would give without pressing for the full sorry tale.

Eleanor settled back in the cramped stage. It was going to be a lonely journey.

*

Lydia had had an unproductive day. Joseph had seemed preoccupied and had been a lacking companion; she was sorely disappointed in him. Of all four men she was considering, he was by far the most handsome; a pity he was not also rich and titled.

She returned home in the foulest of moods, hoping to pour out her troubles to Eleanor. Her mood did not improve when she was told her friend had returned home suddenly due to a family crisis. She cursed Eleanor for leaving her at a time when she needed her the most.

After a lot of cursing and muttering, Lydia sent a letter for hand delivery. It was time she made a decision.

*

Joseph saw Lydia the following day in the Pump Rooms. He had gone alone; Percy was escorting his aunt and was due to join him later, while Archie had expressed the desire to go for a ride alone. Archie's coolness towards him made Joseph wary of what had gone on in the phaeton with Eleanor. Something was definitely amiss, and he needed to speak to Eleanor to find out why she thought he had erred. He was convinced she did, and it was sending him into a blind panic.

He approached Lydia, noticing Sir Ralph and Lady Moore talking animatedly nearby. Joseph bowed to Lydia, noticing she looked annoyed.

"Good morning, Lady Lydia; I hope I find you well?" Joseph asked, resisting the urge to ask immediately after Eleanor.

"I am very well," Lydia said, a little snappishly. She was still unhappy he had failed to come up to scratch.

"I hope Miss Johnson has recovered from her headache?" he asked, ignoring her tone, but noticing that when she was annoyed, her mouth pinched and her features lost their youthful charm. He had the feeling he was seeing the woman she would become. In his opinion, Percy and Archie were fools if they continued to pursue her.

"I have no idea; she decided it was a good idea to return home, some family issue or other. She never even said goodbye," Lydia said, pouting with annoyance.

Joseph's heart sank; there was no family issue, he was sure of it. "I'm sorry to hear that."

"Well, it makes no odds; I am betrothed now, so we shall be busy planning my wedding," Lydia said triumphantly.

"May I wish you happy? Who is the lucky man?" Joseph asked, immediately guessing that Sir Ralph had secured her.

Lydia was annoyed by the lack of expected remorse from Joseph. She had hoped the least he would do would be to look crestfallen, but he appeared pleased at the news. His expression caused her to be more revealing than was wise.

"I have to say, Mr Heaton, I was disappointed in the three of you," Lydia said.

"Oh? I had supposed that Percy and Archie made some sort of promise to you; they certainly seemed to be waiting for an answer from you about something," Joseph replied, correctly guessing both his friends had declared themselves to her

"They did, but their prospects weren't up to scratch. I have been very disappointed. You all dress as if you have large incomes, but from what you've said, there isn't a decent income among you!" Lydia's words were completely inappropriate, but anger and disgust at the way Sir Ralph had kissed her when he had been left alone with her for half an hour the previous evening, made her disregard all sense of propriety.

"So, you were looking for a title and a large fortune," Joseph said, disgust at how mercenary she was proving to be written all over his face.

"I deserve to be married well," Lydia snapped.

"And you would have been if you had chosen either of my friends," Joseph said. "We've just been using our family names in an effort to escape women like yourself who just want a title and fortune rather than the man himself."

"What do you mean?" Lydia gasped, hoping she had misunderstood his meaning.

"Percy is a Viscount and has five thousand a year at his disposal, and Archie is a Baron, with three thousand a year," Joseph said, for once enjoying the look of horror on Lydia's face. "You see, my dear, if you had chosen one of them, you would have been settled for life with someone young, attractive, rich, titled and who worshipped you. Good luck with Sir Ralph; I have known of him although never met him until my excursion into Bath. I wouldn't become too accustomed to his yearly income; he likes to gamble a little too much."

"They lied to me!" Lydia hissed.

"No, they were looking for someone who wanted them, not their money—a feeling I share wholeheartedly," Joseph replied without feeling.

"And you?" Lydia could not resist torturing herself even further.

"Me? I will keep that to myself for now; I don't wish to totally spoil your day," he replied, bowing and turning on his heel. He would hopefully never see such a callous, calculating woman again for a long time.

Chapter 8

Eleanor's lie about returning for a family crisis turned out to be true in some respects; her sister, Grace, was seriously ill when Eleanor arrived at Sudworth Hall. So, instead of wallowing in self-pity, she was kept busy with Grace's illness. Grace had also fallen in love with the Head Gardener which complicated matters.

Rosalind and Peter had dismissed the gardener, but with Eleanor's persuasion, Grace's insistence when she regained consciousness and the interference of a close family friend, they agreed to do what Grace wanted and allowed her to marry her gardener. The family decided their father should only find out after the marriage had taken place, otherwise he would forbid it. Luckily for Rosalind she had married an even tempered man in the Duke of Sudworth, but he was no pushover and wrote to Mr Johnson a letter that would hopefully result in at least some of Grace's dowry being forthcoming. No-one expected Mr Johnson would be magnanimous enough to allow her to have the full dowry she would have received if she had married a titled gentleman.

Eleanor had been kept occupied, so it was two weeks before she could dwell on what had happened in Bath. She cursed herself for being such a fool in believing someone like Joseph could fall in love with her. She knew without a doubt she had fallen in love with him, which made her feel lonely and bereft, difficult to hide in a busy household.

She busied herself in getting to know the Duke's sister, Annie. She was two and twenty, but had a condition that made her look different with her protruding, lidless-looking eyes and thick tongue as well as having the mentality of a child. Eleanor, like the other Johnson girls was to find Annie easy to love. She was moving into the Dower House once the visitor who was staying there had moved out. Rosalind had explained it was to hopefully give Annie some independence while still living within the grounds of the Hall with her companion.

Eleanor had also been introduced to Mrs Adams. She was an elderly lady, who had been best friends with Peter and Annie's mother. She was a plain-speaking tyrant when she wanted to be but had helped the family through their trials and was loyal to them. Eleanor liked the abrupt way Mrs Adams spoke, but she was also wary; Mrs Adams had made some comment on their first meeting as if she suspected what Eleanor was feeling.

Eleanor joined morning visits with Rosalind, wanting to support her sister now that Grace was married and settled in her cottage in the grounds with Harry Long the Head Gardener. Rosalind had been the victim of the gossips since she married Peter; it had not been an easy integration into the community, but her rank and her natural poise and control had given her the strength to remain strong throughout each ordeal. It had cemented the affection the Duke and Duchess felt for each other; a fortunate occurrence as they had been strangers when they married. It had also secured the friendship between Mrs Adams and the new Duchess.

During the third week of Eleanor's visit, Mrs Adams entered the drawing room at the end of visiting time, as she usually did. This way she could spend some time with Annie, who did not like strangers and could not deal confidently with social situations.

Once the pleasantries had been gone through and the last visitor left, Mrs Adams turned to Rosalind with excitement. "I never thought planning a marriage could be so enjoyable," she said with a wide smile.

"Oh?" Rosalind asked with her own smile.

"Stuart and Frances are so amenable to everything I say, it would be sickening if I wasn't enjoying it so much," Mrs Adams explained. Her son had been a tutor for Lord Stannage's family, travelling across Europe with a young man who lived with the Earl's family. When he returned to the family, Lord Stannage had been visiting with his new wife, the second Johnson girl, Annabelle. The couple had not had a promising start to their marriage, and Miss Frances Latimer had been invited to visit. That visit had resulted in Mr Adams declaring his feelings for her and, after some misunderstandings, they finally reached a happy conclusion. Mrs Adams was ecstatic her son was to marry and return home to live.

"We are happy Sudworth Hall is to hold the wedding breakfast; we need more celebrations, although I do think Frances is a brave girl, coming to live with you," Rosalind could not resist teasing. They were both aware of the kind nature of Miss Latimer.

Mrs Adams laughed. "She's only one of a handful who would be brave enough to stand up to me," she admitted. "Which is why she would be perfect for Stuart; I couldn't stand if he had married an empty-headed weakling."

"Frances is quiet but no push-over," Rosalind admitted. "I shall never forget when she slapped Lady Joan across the face. I'm still not quite sure who was the most shocked, Joan or the onlookers."

Mrs Adams chuckled, "Yes, it was the first time anyone had stood up to Joan; should have been done years ago."

*

Rosalind received a letter from her sister, Annabelle later that day explaining they had returned from visiting her husband's family in Carlisle and were at what was to be their principle home, Stannage House, only six miles away from Sudworth Hall.

"Annabelle seems well settled with Lord Stannage now," Rosalind said, after reading the letter. "It seems we Johnson women have to go through a shaky start to find the man we love. When is your heart to be damaged before you have your happy ever after Eleanor?"

Eleanor stiffened but tried to hide it; Rosalind was only teasing, after all. "Oh, I think I shall spend some time with you and then return home to my fate with Mr Wadeson," she replied easily enough.

A frown crossed Rosalind's face. "I don't like to think of you marrying him. Grace especially never takes anyone in dislike, but she is adamant he is not a good man. Myself and Annabelle were lucky in finding men who, although strangers when we married, were good men. I can't see that being the case with Mr Wadeson from what Annabelle and Grace have said."

"Don't worry about me; thanks to Peter, I don't have to rush home," Eleanor responded. It was true; Peter had been assertive when informing her father she had come for a visit. He said she would be returned only after Rosalind's confinement, being insistent Rosalind needed support through the latter stages of her pregnancy and when the infant was newly born. He had extended invitations to Mr and Mrs Johnson to come and visit and care for their eldest daughter, knowing full well that any request for help would fall on deaf ears. Neither parent would wish to have to spend time supporting any of their children. So, with anticipation, the three sisters residing at Sudworth Hall impatiently waited for the arrival of the fourth sister.

Lord Stannage, the Earl of Garston had agreed to a visit to Sudworth Hall; he was aware how much the four sisters thought of each other, and it would be more convenient than travelling to and from his own household each day. The plan pleased Rosalind immensely. Having been a substitute mother for her sisters, she was keen to see them settled around her. She just had to find a husband for Eleanor who lived nearby and then her life would be complete, but for now she could relax, knowing Eleanor was to stay until after the baby had arrived and her confinement ended.

Annabelle and Frederick stepped down from their coach and into the arms of the waiting people. Even Annie had come to greet them. Frederick was introduced to Eleanor, although with the noise going on around them, they would have to wait to exchange anything other than the briefest of pleasantries. With lots of chatter Rosalind managed to move the party inside.

Peter and Frederick stood near the fireplace watching the chattering women as they talked ten to the dozen, asking questions and supplying news. Peter smiled and shook his head at Frederick. "I never expected this house to resound with such happy sounds as it does today. I wish my mother could have seen it."

Frederick nodded his head in understanding. "I will always be grateful your family was in such financial difficulties you were forced to marry a Johnson girl."

Peter laughed, not minding the mention of his deceased brother and father, who between them had driven the estate to near bankruptcy. "I thank my lucky stars every morning and evening," he said, his tone turning serious for a moment. "They have affected so many people in such a positive way, and yet they are still met with derision from some in the locality."

"We have both kept supplying news for the gossips unfortunately," Frederick said, referring to being caught in a compromising position.

"We do. I suppose you heard about Grace?" Peter asked.

"Annabelle told me; she looks happy enough," Frederick said, looking over at the petite sister. She was so much smaller in height and build than her sisters she looked even smaller than she actually was. She would always be the quieter one of the sisters, but she interrupted when she had something to say. Both men noticed, whenever Grace did speak, all the sisters listened to her; it was as if with her not speaking as often, they thought what she had to say was doubly important.

The door opened and an uncomfortable looking Harry walked in. The Head Gardener might never feel comfortable taking part in life at the front of the house. Grace looked up as he entered, and the smile that broke out on her face made her glow. She stood to greet him and brought him into the throng. He looked helplessly at Peter and Frederick and both smiled in sympathy; they were safe near the fireplace; they were not about to sacrifice themselves for the sake of Harry's comfort.

The party was interrupted once again when Bryant announced Mrs Adams and her son and his wife-to-be had arrived. The three newcomers were welcomed into the room.

Mrs Adams took in the crowded drawing room and broke into a smile. "I have finally got a group of people around me who are intelligent enough to raise the quality of society in the area."

"Praise indeed," Rosalind teased. "And you will have a new daughter soon to provide you with company while at home," she said smiling at Frances.

"I'm still worried about living with Mrs Adams," Frances said with a laugh and a blush. "She has terrified me for most of my life!"

"You have enough sense to keep this boy of mine in check and enough backbone that, when needed, you will do the same for me," Mrs Adams said honestly, but her eyes were sparkling with pleasure at Frances standing up to her. She respected few people, but the quiet Frances had shown strength of character the older woman could admire.

"I'd like to witness that happening," Annabelle said, which set the rest of the group laughing at Mrs Adams's mock stern look.

Mr Adams was introduced to everyone before joining Peter and Frederick; this time Harry managed to join them as well. "They terrify me," Harry said, his usual reticence giving way to the feeling of being overwhelmed that had encompassed him since he had walked in the room. It did not help that he was a member of staff, but yet the husband of the Duchess's sister, a combination that put him above the other servants but not quite in the front of house. The family were doing all they could to welcome him, but they knew it would take time before he felt comfortable.

"They terrify us all," Peter replied with a smile. "If we didn't love them, I would suggest we flee, but my wife assures me they are kind to those they care for."

"Congratulations on your engagement," Harry said to Stuart; he knew him a little, as they had both lived within two miles of each other for their whole lives.

"Thank you," Stuart replied. "I didn't think it was going to happen for a long time, but we've sorted out our misunderstandings and, I think, or I hope there will be nothing else to cause us difficulties before the wedding day."

"This year has been quite hectic," Peter said with feeling. "I truly hope next year will be different."

"As fatherhood is imminent, I can't see that happening," Frederick said drily.

"No, and there's the need to try and find a husband for Eleanor," Peter said. "Rosalind will never forgive me if I encourage a marriage to someone who lives more than a few hours travel away. The only problem is we are running out of single men!"

*

Peter received a letter the following morning that surprised and intrigued him. He waited until he could speak to Rosalind alone, as the contents had to be treated carefully. He eventually found her resting in her bedchamber. During late afternoon she would often go for a lie-down. Now she was near the end of her pregnancy, she tired easier.

She smiled as Peter walked into the room. "Hello, have you come to join me?" Rosalind asked, patting the bed beside her.

Peter was sorely tempted, but he resisted. "I need to speak to you in confidence about a letter I received this morning," he said, sitting next to her.

"Oh?" Rosalind said, sitting up. "What is it?"

"I think you'd better read this, but before I hand it to you, I need you to promise you won't mention its contents to anyone, especially your sisters," Peter said firmly.

Rosalind frowned. "Of course," she said, reaching for the letter. She did not recognise the hand it was written in so began reading with interest.

Dear Peter,

It is a long time since our paths have crossed—too many years for me to admit to—but I am writing to you for help. Before I ask for your support, I feel I need to offer some information as background. Please be assured that I have not spoken to another living soul about this, and I would be grateful for your confidence in the matter.

You know my position in life, as you are fully aware that position comes with its good points as well as bad. I was sick of the marriage mart that is the season and decided I was going to accompany some friends, who were in a similar situation, and visit Bath. We used our family names and luckily because most of the population in Bath were older than us, we were never discovered.

You remember Percy West? Well, he was already residing there and chasing a chit of the Moore family. Myself and Archie set off with the aim of giving Lady Lydia two more dandies to dance with and give Percy a run for his money. I wish it had turned out so simply.

A Miss Eleanor Johnson was staying with Lady Lydia and from the start I...well let's just say, I had never met anyone like her. She was unaffected, funny, and completely honest about her situation and her outlook on life. Every time we met, I was drawn to her, until I was sure I had found someone whom I could spend the rest of my days with.

For the first time in my life I was thinking I would be seeking her out to offer for her, but some words I said foolishly before our trip came back to haunt me. I had told Archie that, when chasing a pretty woman, you should always make a fuss of the plain friend in order to gain credibility with the one you are really chasing. I don't need to add what happened, do I? Those words, said in a moment of arrogance will haunt me for the rest of my days. Miss Johnson believes I consider her the plain friend and that I've used her ill.

Believe me, I consider her the most intriguing, appealing, mesmerising woman I have ever met. To me she is beautiful, but I know she would not believe that. She once said when one has always been introduced as the intelligent one, it is obvious that good looks are not a consideration. So, this along with my words being repeated to her sent her from Bath quicker than I could rectify the situation.

I am desperate to see her, to make things right with her and try to receive her forgiveness. She mentioned her eldest sister was your wife, and I wonder if you could be imposed upon to ask her to visit you for a while. I have not told her who I am, so she never guessed there could be a connection between the two of us, although I know it is loose.

You owe me no special favours, and I would not be asking if I was not desperate to make amends. All I can do is impose on your good nature and ask for your help. I say this praying her father has not already forced her into a marriage with someone else.

Yours in desperation

Joseph Heaton

"Well!" Rosalind spluttered after reading the letter fully through twice. "Eleanor was keeping a secret and never said a word! Oh, she must have been mortified, the poor girl. What a brute he must be to have said such a thing!"

"He admits it was bravado in front of a friend. I know the three of them; we were at school together: all are decent men," Peter said defending his long-ago school chums.

"Poor Eleanor," Rosalind said, looking over the letter once more. "We were always introduced in a certain way, but she missed the point; none of us was introduced as the pretty one. I was the motherly one, not very complimentary when you are still in the school room! Annabelle was the mischievous one, Grace the gardening one and Eleanor the intelligent one."

"We all know how words can be misunderstood," Peter said pointedly.

Rosalind flushed, being reminded of the time when she had thought Peter did not wish to have children, and she had tried to hide that she was increasing, almost returning home to her parents. "I suppose so," she admitted. "He speaks highly of Eleanor; have you seen how he describes her? If she saw this, she would be under no doubt he had feelings for her."

"We are not going to show this to Eleanor," Peter said firmly. "I will write to Joe and offer accommodation for him for as long as he wishes. I will help him, as he has asked, but it is up to him to apologise and receive forgiveness from Eleanor. They need to see each other, so the misunderstanding can be cleared fully for them to have any chance at anything else."

Rosalind accepted what Peter said with a nod and then she smiled. "My little Eleanor has fallen in love," she said, ever the proud substitute mother.

"But she has also been hurt," Peter reminded her.

"I know. I wish she had confided in one of us; we could have helped, but I suppose this way, she will be certain there hasn't been any interference from any of us. Is Mr Heaton a good man?" Rosalind asked.

Peter smiled, "You have no idea who he is, have you?"

"No," Rosalind admitted.

"Percy and Archie are a Viscount and Baron; it was obvious from what Joe said they were sick of being chased for their titles. I'm surprised they got away with it, but the fact that he is certain Eleanor doesn't know his identity convinces me they did," Peter said with wonder.

"So he has a title? It means father will be pleased if she does forgive him," Rosalind said.

"Oh yes, he'll be pleased; Mr Joseph Heaton is the Duke of Adlington," Peter said with a broad grin.

"He's a Duke, and she doesn't know?" Rosalind squeaked. "But he has mentioned her background, so he must know that father is in business."

"Yes, he must and what's more, even if your father lost all his money tomorrow, Joe wouldn't worry; his estate is one of the richest in the country. If she marries him, your father's dowry will be nothing more than pin money," Peter informed his wife.

In true Rosalind style, she pooh-poohed the money aspect of it. "If he loves her, she won't care what money he brings; I hope he turns out to be good enough for her. I only want the best type of man for my baby sister."

Chapter 9

Peter announced they were going to be having another visitor in a few days. Rosalind and Peter watched Eleanor closely when Peter referred to the Duke of Adlington, but there was no recognition or impact on Eleanor's demeanour at all. It was obvious she did not connect the Duke with the man she left behind in Bath.

On the third day, after the arrival of the letter, Peter received the expected visitor. Joseph was shown into Peter's study.

"Good morning," Peter said, rising from the seat behind his desk. "Have you had a good journey?"

"It's been a fast one," Joseph admitted. "I rode with my valet; my carriage and further luggage is travelling separately."

"Keen to get here?" Peter asked with a smile.

"Desperate more than anything," Joseph admitted, rubbing his hand through his hair. "I can't tell you of the range of emotions I've been feeling since she left."

"I have some understanding," Peter admitted, without going into detail. "Eleanor returned to us; she did not travel to her parents."

"I admit to not being surprised," Joseph acknowledged. "From what she said, I don't feel any of her sisters had a close relationship with their parents."

"No, they are a close unit as sisters, but when we first married I was surprised how little my wife was in contact with either of her parents," Peter said.

At that moment Rosalind entered the room and was introduced to Joseph. "Welcome to our home," Rosalind said, trying to assess the man before her.

"Thank you and thank you for your support," Joseph said with feeling.

"Everyone deserves a chance to make amends, but if Eleanor does not forgive you, you shall receive no further support from me. I will always put my sister first," Rosalind said, not unkindly but wishing to be clear with the man before her. She had only Peter's word he was a good man and, although that carried some weight, he had to prove he was good enough for Eleanor.

"I would expect nothing else," Joseph said with a slight bow. "I am grateful you have given me this opportunity."

"I told you they were a force to be reckoned with," Peter said with a smile. "If you are successful, you will be hen-pecked for the rest of your days."

"I would welcome it; anything to move this feeling of loss," Joseph said seriously.

It was decided Peter would introduce Joseph to the wider party after morning visits, giving Joseph enough time to refresh himself and ensuring there would be fewer interruptions.

The four Johnson sisters sat around the fireplace, with Annie, Frances and Mrs Adams after visits had been completed. They were talking about the wedding of Frances and Stuart when Peter walked in. He was thankful Eleanor had her back to him; it would give him an extra moment or two before Eleanor realised what was afoot.

"Rosalind, may I introduce the Duke of Adlington to you?" Joseph stepped forward, aware there were a large number of eyes turned in his direction, but he was interested in only one pair.

Rosalind acted as if she had never met Joseph, welcoming him to her home and then introducing him to the gathered women. Her heart squeezed uncomfortably when she saw the paleness of Eleanor's complexion and the hurt in her eyes, but Rosalind had agreed to the scheme, so she had to see it through.

Eleanor could not comprehend at first what was happening. Joseph stood in front of her, but being introduced as a Duke? Her mind raced trying to make sense of it while fighting with the feelings his presence caused. Her stomach had reacted on instinct first of all, flipping with pleasure before the hurt rose to the surface, suppressing any pleasant feelings.

It must be another lie, she decided, but then realised he must be telling the truth; Peter would never be involved with lies. She curtseyed when it was her turn to be introduced, but she did not meet his eyes.

"Miss Johnson, it is a pleasure to meet you again," Joseph said, bowing to her curtsey.

"I'm sorry; you are mistaken: we haven't met. I would have remembered the Duke of Adlington, I'm sure," Eleanor replied stiffly before sitting down and picking up her tea cup. The dregs of tea remaining were cold and almost made her shudder, but she managed to maintain her poise while the other introductions were being made.

When Eleanor looked up, she met the assessing look of Mrs Adams. Eleanor smiled a little and shrugged her shoulders. Rosalind had told Eleanor of the help Mrs Adams had provided in sorting out the troubles Rosalind and Peter had faced, but Eleanor did not want Mrs Adams to interfere. She could never trust Joseph again.

Within a few moments, Eleanor excused herself from the room. Joseph followed her with his eyes, desperate to go after her and try to explain but unable to. Mrs Adams stood, indicating that Frances should join her. There was obviously something going on they weren't aware of, so it was time to leave the family alone. She was sure more would be revealed as time progressed.

Joseph took a walk around the grounds during the afternoon. He was beginning to think his decision might have been a mistake; Eleanor had not joined the group for lunch, claiming a headache. He never thought she would withdraw from him. He cursed himself; he was a fool.

Walking through an archway that led into a rose garden he almost collided with Eleanor. He reached out to steady her, but she pulled back from him as if stung.

"Miss Johnson, please allow me to have a word with you; I need to explain myself," Joseph said, quickly trying to use the situation to his advantage.

Eleanor looked at the man before her before speaking. "Who are you?" she asked. "Did anything you said hold any truth in it? You weren't even honest about who you were."

"It did with relation to you," Joseph said. "We had been sickened by the constant chasing having a title and fortune brings, so we decided we would go somewhere we had never been before and pretend to be normal human beings."

"But you were lying to everyone and very convincingly," Eleanor willed herself to walk away, but part of her wanted to know why he had carried out such a scheme.

"It was my idea," Joseph admitted. It was important for him to be truthful from now on, no matter what the consequences were. "I was becoming sick of society and its falseness. I needed to reassure myself there were decent people around."

His voice sounded sincere, but Eleanor reminded herself he had sounded sincere on other occasions. "And you found Lydia and myself enough to send you reeling from society for good," Eleanor responded with derision. "If you would excuse me, I need to return to the hall."

She walked through the archway, but Joseph followed her. "Eleanor, please, what Archie told you was wrong."

"You didn't say it?" Eleanor asked, looking back over her shoulder but not stopping.

"I did, but it was not aimed at you; I didn't even know you then! I was just being an arrogant fool!" Joseph said.

Eleanor stopped walking and turned to face him. "Do you think it would make it any better to know the words were not aimed specifically at me? It was aimed at all the people who are not quite as pretty as their more popular friends. How do you think anyone would feel being used to gain favour in conquering their friend? Is that the behaviour of a true gentleman of any rank? I think not! I would never have thought you could be so cruel or calculating, but for many days I have come to realise you and Lady Lydia deserve each other. I could think of no-one better for either of you."

Eleanor did not wait for a response; she resumed the walk that would eventually lead her to the sanctuary of her bedchamber. She was aware she could not hide there forever, but for now she needed solace.

Joseph watched her retreating figure. He was not sure whether to follow her, but he decided against it. If he forced her to listen to him, neither of them would receive any satisfaction from the conversation. He would falter through panic at wanting to make things right, and she would not really listen to him. He did not know what to do, but he knew that to push things further at the moment would not help his cause.

They met again at the evening meal. Joseph was to realise what a unique family he had become embroiled in when sitting at the same dining table were two dukes, a lord who had different coloured eyes, a tutor and a gardener. Mrs Adams, Frances and Stuart had also joined the family for the evening. Joseph found the grouping novel and reassuring; there were no airs and graces: the family just accepted everyone for who they were.

He was not seated near Eleanor, but he was next to Rosalind. He was grateful when she brought up the topic of Eleanor. "I hope you have patience; my sister may not forgive so easily."

"I have already guessed that; I just hope she will speak to me. I think through time she will be convinced I didn't intend hurting anyone, especially her," Joseph said with feeling.

"She's not one who holds a grudge unnecessarily; it will be down to how convincing or should I say how truthful you are from now on," Rosalind advised.

"I have already been truthful with her; but it did not end well: she condemned me further," Joseph replied with a grimace.

Rosalind laughed, "If she cares for you, she will forgive. None of us stays angry for long."

"I hope not, or I may have to kidnap her," Joseph said with a smile.

Rosalind ignored the comment; she took it for the jest it was. She decided to find out a little more about the man. "I've no idea where your estate is; you will find me lacking in knowledge of who is located where in the aristocracy. It comes of being raised outside the ton."

"My main residence is near Shrewsbury, about a day's drive with a good carriage and team of horses. I also have a house in London and a small estate on Anglesey. I love the rugged coastline of the island."

"Oh, a day away isn't too far," Rosalind said, more to herself than to Joseph. She would have preferred a closer location, but understood that, if they were to marry eventually, a day away was not too restricting.

"No. I've also been thinking of buying some land on the Cheshire plains, so even closer," Joseph said with a smile, guessing some of what Rosalind was thinking.

"Better and better," Rosalind said with a smile.

Later when the ladies withdrew from the dining room Rosalind had the opportunity to speak to Eleanor. She tried to make light of the situation; Eleanor had obviously not wanted to confide, and Rosalind had to respect that. "Well you have managed to outdo us all," she said with a smile.

"How's that?" Eleanor asked warily.

"To get a duke to fall in love with you, just for being you," Rosalind said.

"I got a duke to lie, insult and use me, nothing more," Eleanor said sharply.

"My mistake," Rosalind said, moving away. "He talks about you as if he is in love with you."

Eleanor was not unfeeling enough not to be affected by Rosalind's words. She cursed that her sister had probably said the words purposely to stir her curiosity, and she cursed her own vanity. She sat down but was not to be left alone; Mrs Adams came to join her.

"So, I presume you met this young man of yours in Bath?" Mrs Adams asked, as always coming directly to the point.

"He is not my young man but, yes, I was introduced to the man he was pretending to be during my stay in Bath," Eleanor replied tersely.

"Intrigue as well! I shall watch with interest," Mrs Adams said chuckling.

"You will be very disappointed," Eleanor said, determined she was not going to be forced into doing anything she did not want to do just to provide entertainment for those inclined to waste their time watching her.

"If I had someone watching me as he watches you, I'd be thinking very seriously before rejecting him. Passion like that doesn't come by very often, but I'm an old interfering woman, so what do I know?" Mrs Adams said, rising from her seat with the aid of her stick. She had done what she had wanted to; there was no future in belabouring the point; the girl would make her own decision.

Eleanor felt slightly cornered, but she was intelligent enough to listen to the advice given. Rosalind would never promote someone she found lacking, although to be fair, Eleanor had not told her the extent of

Joseph's insult. She also trusted the judgement of Mrs Adams even though their acquaintance was brief, but she was still hurting, and that could also not be ignored.

Joseph wisely judged that to approach Eleanor in the drawing room would not earn him any favours. He sat near Grace and her ever attentive husband Harry. Grace was welcoming, although Harry was quiet.

"My mother says Bath isn't the fashionable place it used to be, Your Grace. Did you find it lacking?" Grace asked.

"I tend to use my family name, Heaton; I am not one for such formalities," Joseph explained. "It's not as it once was; everyone who is anyone stays in Brighton now, but I find sometimes an escape to a familiar place is almost as good as exploring a new place."

"Oh, have you been before?" Grace queried.

"A long time ago, not since I was quite young. Then it was the place to be seen, my parents enjoyed their trips there." Joseph turned to Harry. "Mr Long, I believe I should seek your advice on something, if you are willing?"

"I shall do what I can to help, but it is Harry, Your Grace," Harry said, always aware he did not really fit into the social circle.

"It is Harry as long as I am Joseph," came the firm reply. "I refuse to allow you to give me the respect of my station if I can't give you yours."

Harry nodded in acceptance. "How can I help you, Joseph?" he asked with a small smile.

"I have been considering buying a property on the Cheshire plains, but I'm a little wary about flooding. I was hoping to have gardens that would be best suited to that type of land and potentially could help to prevent the flooding in the first place, if that is possible? I will be employing someone but, if I take advice first, at least I will know who is speaking the truth when I interview them," Joseph explained. "I will pay for your time of course."

"There is no need for payment," Harry said sharply.

"Oh, I think there is," Joseph responded firmly. "I will be asking for a lot of your time during the evenings when you have finished work. If payment is an issue, we can forget the conversation, and I will seek advice from someone who is willing to be recompensed for their knowledge. You have a speciality, Harry; make it work for you. You are married to a woman who has a businessman as a father; he would advise you to do the same."

"He would. He's always on the lookout for the next scheme," Grace said. She turned to Harry and squeezed his hand. "Mr Heaton is correct in what he says; you have a talent Harry: use it to our advantage."

"I will help you," Harry said gruffly; he still could not refuse his beautiful wife anything.

"Thank you, I appreciate it," Joseph responded, feeling a little intrusive and jealous at the closeness and the looks the couple were exchanging.

He excused himself and joined Peter near the window. Peter indicated Grace and Harry. "It's a little overwhelming to see isn't it?" He had correctly understood Joseph's reaction.

"I envy them," Joseph said honestly.

"I have never seen a man change so much as Harry has done since he met Grace. You may think he is reticent and looks uncomfortable, but only months ago, he would never have uttered a word and would have had to be dragged with a gun against his head before entering into a situation such as this. He adores her and will do anything for her," Peter said, never quite being able to overcome his feelings of wonder over the difference in his gardener.

"They are very lucky," Joseph said.

Peter understood the longing in his voice, but did not comment on it. If he was to be successful with Eleanor, it would be down to his own efforts; it was not right that people interfered. They had provided the platform of opportunity; it was up to the couple to sort out their differences.

Eleanor watched Joseph while they were gathered in the drawing room. She knew she was weak, but could not help being drawn to him even though she still stung from the hurt she felt each time she thought of Bath. He was the first man who had grabbed her attention from the moment she had seen him and, seeing him now with her family, seemed to only increase the torture.

She wanted him to be the man she had thought he was, but it had all been an act, and she had to keep reminding herself of that. He was comfortable in the grouping, and in some ways it was she who felt like the outsider, her insecurities coming to the forefront. Looking around at the group of people, she saw that everyone was happy, everyone secure with who they were and who they loved. She was the outsider, unsure about her future and somehow feeling unsettled.

She needed to rid herself of feelings she could not seem to shake. She refused to feel regret; she had made her decision to offer herself to marry Mr Wadeson, and she would stick to it.

Chapter 10

Eleanor went to visit Grace; she was closer to Grace than her other two sisters purely because they were the two closest in age. She had gone to seek Grace's advice, having had yet another troubled night's sleep.

Grace poured tea and listened as Eleanor unburdened herself. She had not interrupted. Eleanor finished and sat staring forlornly into her cup.

"You have fallen in love with him and still have feelings for him; there is no surprise in that, is there?" Grace asked quietly. "He's a very handsome man."

"Not that I fell in love with him, but how can I still have feelings when he hurt me so much?" Eleanor asked, anguish in her expression. "It doesn't make sense."

"Of course, it does; just because you heard he said some foolish things, you still believe what you saw and heard from him yourself. You still love him because his actions were believable," Grace said reasonably. "Harry has a very strong sense of what is right and wrong; he fought against his feelings, but I never doubted that he loved me: his actions were contradictory to his words."

"I don't know what his intentions were towards Lydia," Eleanor said.

"I think the fact he is here shows he had no intentions towards Lydia at all. If she was as calculating as you describe, I cannot imagine an intelligent man would miss the signs," Grace reasoned.

"Oh! Every time I think about it my head hurts!" Eleanor exclaimed. "And the problem is I'm thinking of nothing else at the moment."

Grace reached over and squeezed Eleanor's hand. "Don't put yourself under so much pressure; there is no hurry. Why not just see what happens while he is staying here?"

"I suppose so," Eleanor said doubtfully. "I veer from wanting to be kissed by him to wanting to strangle him!"

Grace laughed, "I can understand that, but I think Rosalind might be a little upset if you tried to kill one of her guests; she doesn't want any more fuel for the gossips."

Eleanor pondered Grace's words as she returned to the hall. It was always comforting talking to Grace; there was never any pressure from her: she just listened and comforted. Perhaps she was right; there was no rush. In reality, no one but herself was putting any pressure on her.

Joseph noticed Eleanor as she walked and set-out so their paths would cross. If the truth be told, he had been looking for her. He had not spoken to her during the last evening, but he needed to speak to her now. The longing to be near her was almost overwhelming, a strange sensation for one who was used to being in control.

Eleanor looked up, unsurprised to see Joseph striding towards her. He had a look of uncertainty on his face, as if he was unsure of her response. She was not sure herself of how to respond to him, so in some ways she could sympathise with his expression.

"Good morning, Mr Heaton," she said with a curtsey.

"Miss Johnson," he replied with a bow. "May I join you?" Eleanor shrugged; it was not quite the welcome Joseph had hoped for, but it was better than a refusal.

They walked in silence for a few moments before Joseph spoke. "I think Percy is still a little blue he lost out to Sir Ralph."

Eleanor paused in walking. "Lydia has accepted Sir Ralph's proposal?" Her astonishment was clear.

Joseph smiled, "Have you not heard? I thought she would have written her news to you."

"I told them I was returning home; if she sent a letter, my parents may not have thought to forward it on. I'm not really surprised she accepted him; she was determined her future husband had to be titled," Eleanor said walking once more.

"She wasn't very pleased with me the last time we met," Joseph admitted, the familiar twinkle in his eyes.

Eleanor forced herself to concentrate on his words. "She was hoping to receive a proposal from you, then you all would have proposed before she made her decision."

"She was to be disappointed," Joseph replied with firmness. "A proposal from me was never going to be forthcoming. Her arrogance when we met and the fact I was missing you made me a little more callous than I would have been normally."

"Oh?" Eleanor asked, unable to respond to his pointed comment.

"I informed her that, if she was looking for a title, she should have been more patient," Joseph explained. "Percy is a Viscount and has five thousand a year and Archie is a Baron, with three thousand a year. She wasn't very happy."

"Oh, my goodness!" Eleanor exclaimed, trying to hold back a laugh. "Poor Lydia."

"I'm afraid I don't share your sympathies," Joseph responded a little harshly. "Women like her were exactly the reason I fled from London. You could see their aims in the way they could not hide the scheming from their look, or the way they hinted they would be willing for any sort of marriage to take place. Affection and respect were not considerations; the title and fortune were."

"Some would like to have women throw themselves in their paths," Eleanor said reasonably.

"Not me. I would rather die a bachelor than marry on those terms," Joseph responded. "I'm sorry you feel we deceived you by not introducing ourselves honestly; it was my idea to use our family names, but I hope you understand the reason we did it."

"I do," Eleanor acknowledged. Before Lydia revealed her true motivation in seeking marriage, Eleanor would not have believed a young woman could be so mercenary, but Lydia had opened her eyes in a way she had not welcomed. It did make her more sympathetic to that part of the deception, although not all of it. She still stung at the insult about the plain friend. That would not be so easy to forget.

They separated at the Hall, Joseph a little encouraged and Eleanor still as confused. They joined the others for luncheon, gathering around the dining table in a less formal manner than the evening meal dictated.

Eleanor lost her appetite when Bryant interrupted the meal to announce that Mr Johnson had arrived with a Mr Wadeson. Rosalind stood up exclaiming, "Father has arrived? I had no idea he was intending to visit!"

The remaining group looked at each other in shock. It was not the fact Mr Johnson had arrived that caused the stunned silence. Eleanor and Annabelle had lost their colour, looking horrified at the news and, Joseph and Frederick both looked like thunder.

Mrs Adams who was seated with the family looked on with curiosity. Eleanor and Joseph's reaction she could understand; it was common knowledge Mr Wadeson was expected to marry one of the girls and, as Eleanor was the only single one left, it did not take much deduction to realise hers was a look of panic and Joseph's the look of a threatened suitor. The reaction that caused her curiosity was that of Annabelle and Frederick; she wondered what circumstance involved the couple that the remainder of the family were unaware of.

Mr Johnson walked in to the dining room not pausing to greet anyone before speaking. "I thought it was time I visited; goodness knows what has got into you all, but if you thought I would agree to a marriage to a gardener you are much mistaken. I'm not sure what scheme you have planned for Eleanor," he aimed his words at Rosalind. "But I thought I would bring Wadeson here to be married before you decided a footman was good enough for your sister!"

Mr Wadeson looked on in silence, but his demeanour was not pleasant. He looked to be approaching thirty and had a wider girth than looked comfortable, his waistcoat and frock coat straining slightly against his bulk. His eyes were close together and narrowed as he took in the group of people before him. His air was not one of friendliness, which was surprising to those who had never met him before. If he were wishing to marry Eleanor, surely he would try to win favour with the extended family, but instead he stood glowering at them.

*

The silence was broken eventually by Peter standing and moving to greet the unexpected guests. "Mr Johnson, Mr Wadeson, welcome to Sudworth Hall. I hope you had a pleasant journey. Bryant, please have Mrs Dawlish prepare rooms for the gentlemen. In the meantime, would you care to join us for some luncheon?"

The two men were introduced to everyone they were not acquainted with and sat in the new places set-out by the ever efficient footmen. Mr Johnson began to speak once his plate was filled; Peter had wisely dismissed the staff, there being no advantage to giving staff gossip. He was grateful Harry was out working, as the first thing Mr Johnson wished to attack was Grace's marriage.

"What possessed you to agree to the match; your instructions were to get your sisters a titled man!" he said accusingly to Rosalind.

"Rosalind was against the match in the first instance," Peter explained patiently. "But I insisted on the marriage taking place. Grace had been compromised and was going to be ruined by gossip. If anyone is to blame, it is I."

Grace's high opinion of Peter was increased even further at his words and the sly look he gave to her, indicating she should remain quiet. He was taking the blame for the situation willingly, and Grace was touched by the gesture.

"The gossip would have died down," Mr Johnson said dismissively.

"My family has had enough scandal attached to it," Peter said, his voice losing some of its pleasantness. "And I will make decisions that have an impact on my household as I see fit. The last time I looked the marriage agreement between myself and your daughter did not give you any control over decisions that affected my household."

The Johnson girls all stilled, looking to their father to see how he would react at such a speech, but to their surprise and relief Mr Johnson shrugged and continued eating. "It is no problem; I will have the marriage annulled."

Grace gasped with horror and looked to Peter, terrified. Peter smiled a small smile of reassurance to her, before turning back to Mr Johnson. "It will be a little difficult to obtain an annulment when I shall provide a statement that they have been living together for some months."

Peter's words gave Grace the courage she needed; she was supported but, more than that, her life with Harry was being threatened—something she could not accept without a fight. "And I shall provide a statement to say I am increasing with Harry's child, therefore, preventing an annulment taking place."

There were more gasps and then congratulations as the sisters pushed back their chairs in order to embrace Grace. A few minutes passed before the room settled once more, and Mr Johnson turned to his second youngest daughter. "You may think you are clever, but you won't feel so smug when you're living in a cold cottage with a handful of brats, wondering where your next meal is coming from."

A noise from the door drew everyone's attention. Bryant had sent for Harry when the guests had arrived, a butler's sixth sense detecting trouble. Harry entered the room unnoticed and listened to the comments being made. He decided he had heard enough, and it was time to intervene.

"And perhaps you won't feel so smug when you realise your daughter is being well cared for and has enough money to buy anything she may wish for. We don't need your dowry and don't want it. You can keep your money, but if you think I'm going to give up my wife, you will have the biggest fight on your hands you have ever faced."

Mr Johnson admired spirit, especially from a working background. He looked Harry up and down, seeing steel in his eyes. He nodded his head. "I won't contest the marriage, but you won't receive a penny from me."

"Good," Harry growled, before grabbing an empty chair and sitting next to his wife. He might feel uncomfortable, but there was nothing that would have prevented him from supporting Grace at that moment.

The room descended into an uncomfortable silence, everyone waiting for someone else to break the quiet. Bryant was the one to relieve the tension by entering to announce that the rooms for the guests were ready. Mr Johnson stood, indicating that Mr Wadeson should follow.

"We shall freshen up and then I would be obliged if we could speak in private," he said, looking at Peter.

"Of course," Peter replied.

*

Mr Johnson was shown into Peter's study. Peter was seated in one of the winged-backed chairs near the fireplace. He indicated Mr Johnson should join him and offered a glass of brandy, which the gentleman accepted.

"How can I help you?" Peter asked.

"I intend Eleanor to marry Wadeson," Mr Johnson said, coming directly to the point. He was a man who did not believe in any sort of flowery language.

"I believe you originally wanted titles for all of your daughters," Peter said, debating what to mention about Joseph's interest in Eleanor.

"I did but then realised I was effectively handing over a business to Wadeson. It seems only right one of my own benefits beyond a dowry," Mr Johnson explained. "I will always value business over title, although I admit to thinking titles would bring them advantages my business could not."

"You are correct in that assumption," Peter said, choosing not to reveal any difficulties they had faced due to the prejudices because of the connection to a businessman.

"I think if Wadeson had been known to me before I'd married Rosalind off, I would have married her to him and then the others would have been free to marry who they wished, but once I'd started on this scheme, it seemed prudent to see it through."

Peter's stomach had clenched at Mr Johnson's words. Never mind the thought of Rosalind with anyone else made him sick to his stomach, the whole attitude of the man sitting before him sickened him. He was not concerned in the slightest that he was playing with his daughter's lives; he was concerned only with what he thought was a good idea at the time. Peter wondered about his business acumen. How someone could be so successful when he seemed to jump from one scheme to another with hardly a thought to the consequences he had no idea, but successful he was.

"Could I suggest that, instead of rushing into anything, you stay for a visit with us? I know Rosalind is keen to have Eleanor with her until after her confinement," Peter suggested.

"We will stay for a few days," Mr Johnson said. "I have business I want to carry out in Preston; after that is completed I shall return home and take Eleanor with me. She can be married from home; my wife is desirous of organising a wedding."

"She could always visit and arrange the wedding here," Peter suggested. "That way all the sisters could be together."

"My wife would never arrange a wedding here; she would wish to rely on suppliers she is familiar with. No, Eleanor will be married from home," Mr Johnson said firmly. He stood, "I shall leave you now; I wish to spend some time going through paperwork with Wadeson before we travel to Preston tomorrow."

Peter was left feeling a little stunned. It was a miracle any of the four sisters were as well rounded individuals as they were. They obviously were the product of two of the most selfish people he had ever come across. It staggered him that Mr Johnson could so blithely ignore the wishes of any of his daughters. He hoped to goodness he would never treat anyone like that, let alone a family member.

Peter sent a message to Joseph, who soon joined him. "I have some worrying news," Peter said.

"I supposed so," Joseph acknowledged.

"He is determined Eleanor will marry Mr Wadeson, whatever her thoughts or feelings on the matter. I thought it appropriate not to mention your interest in his daughter. I feel if he suspects anything he will return home with her immediately, whether you are a duke or a pauper. I thought to encourage him to stay for a while; luckily enough he wants to carry out some business in Preston, so our location is to his advantage. It will give you a little longer to persuade Eleanor, although to what end I don't really know."

Joseph sat quietly for a few moments. "If he won't be persuaded away from this Wadeson character it seems pointless I even try. It would seem to just increase both our suffering if I manage to obtain her forgiveness and then she is taken away from me in the end."

"I understand," Peter said with sympathy. "It was the best I could do, I'm afraid."

"It's not your fault; you have been supportive beyond what I had hoped, and I thank you. I just wish my timing was better," Joseph said with feeling. "Damn it!"

Peter left Joseph alone to mull over his options. He did not envy the man but could not see how he could overcome Mr Johnson's determination to see his daughter married to the man he had chosen for her.

Chapter 11

Annabelle asked Rosalind and Eleanor to accompany her to Grace's cottage the following afternoon. She had tossed and turned and discussed everything with Frederick, and they decided that this was the best course of action.

She kept the chatter light as the three of them walked through the grounds to the small, but neat cottage that belonged to the Head Gardener. Since marrying Harry, Grace had turned the cottage into a home rather than a house lived in by an unmarried man. She made cushions and added throws and lace to surfaces, repainting some of the walls and adding shelves for books. Flowers brightened every room, brought home every night by a doting husband.

Grace had the tea service ready and was taking scones out of the oven as the three arrived. They sniffed the fragrance with pleasure before gathering around the large, well-scrubbed table that filled the centre of the room.

"I need to straighten one thing out before we find out why Annabelle has gathered us in so much secrecy," Grace started, her face colouring with a blush.

"Oh?" Rosalind said with interest, still focusing on the warm scones.

"I'm not really increasing; at least I don't think I am," Grace blurted out in a rush. She sat as if the words had been a relief to say.

"What? Why did you say it then?" Annabelle asked, stunned.

"It was the only thing I could think of that would put paid to father's scheme to annul the marriage," Grace said smiling sheepishly.

"Good ploy!" Eleanor said with approval. "But what are you going to do when no child arrives at the expected month?"

"Oh, I expect father will have completely forgotten by then," Grace said with a grin. "You know how he becomes absorbed in his work. He will forget about dates, and I was quite clear with Harry last night. I told him he better get his act together and produce a child, or there would be trouble!"

Eleanor and Annabelle looked stunned for a second before roaring with laughter at the outrageous comment from their quiet sister. Grace beamed at them both but then noticed Rosalind had her head in her hands, visibly shaking.

"Rosalind?" Grace asked tentatively, the last thing she wanted to do was to upset Rosalind.

Rosalind looked up with tears of laughter in her eyes, "Oh, my baby girl, what has become of you?" she said before reaching over and embracing her. "I'm sure one of you will be the death of me!"

When the laughter eventually died down, they feasted on scones and tea. Annabelle waited until they were all settled comfortably. She knew what she had to say would be upsetting and had wanted to enjoy the visit before telling her story.

Annabelle took a breath; she had come with a set purpose in mind, and it was time to get on with it. "I need to tell you all something I hope you will keep confidential, until father has left at least," she started.

"What is it?" Rosalind asked, immediately alert at the change in Annabelle's demeanour.

Annabelle looked down, not wanting to look at any of them. She was sure there would not be, but she could not bear to see the look of disgust on their faces; she took a few deep breaths: it was time to be brave. She looked at her sisters with tears in her eyes. "I need another promise, and I will explain in a moment: none of you, married or not—because I don't think it would matter to him either way—must be alone with Mr Wadeson."

All three were immediately serious and alert to what Annabelle was saying. Annabelle reached over and took Eleanor's hand in her own. "You are the one most at risk, Eleanor; he will be looking for opportunities to be with you. Please don't put yourself in a position where you will be private with him."

"I won't," Eleanor said quietly. "What has he done to you, Annabelle?"

Annabelle's tears spilled onto her cheeks at the sympathetic words. "He is cruel and brutal."

Rosalind was feeling a rushing sensation in her ears, but she forced herself to concentrate on Annabelle. Her sister needed her strength, all of their strengths now, and she was not going to let her down.

Eleanor did not need a looking glass to know the colour had drained from her face, but she tried to sound calm when she spoke. "What did he do, Annabelle?"

Annabelle turned to Grace. "I am so sorry; I couldn't tell you, and I left you in a potentially horrific situation. I will never forgive myself for that."

Grace leaned across and squeezed Annabelle's free hand. "He did not approach me; he was absent from the house for a while after you left. I never thought anything of it, just appreciated that he wasn't there. You have nothing to apologise for."

"He didn't touch you? Are you being truthful Grace?" Annabelle said, begging her sister to tell her the truth.

"He didn't," Grace said firmly. "Tell us," she said gently.

"I think I was a bit of a challenge to him," she started slowly. "My mouth getting me into more trouble than I could handle. I used to think I was so confident, but in reality I was as frightened as a child when it came down to it."

Annabelle sat up a little straighter. "I never liked him; the way he looked at me made my skin crawl, but he always seemed to want to verbally spar with me, and I, like a fool, I obliged him every time."

"Do you remember the night you accompanied mother to the theatre, and I wasn't feeling well?" Annabelle asked Grace.

"Yes, you had worsened when we had returned; I regretted leaving you alone," Grace replied.

"I didn't feel well because that morning I had taken something over to father's office. I hadn't minded; I liked walking through the factory, the noises and the people I loved, but when I reached the office father wasn't there, just Mr Wadeson. He started talking to me and walked around me, locking the office door. I foolishly thought it was some sort of joke, but then he grabbed me and threw me against the drawers," Annabelle said with a shudder.

"I lost my breath for a moment, and he used it to his full advantage. He pinned me up against the wall with my hair, and he forced my face around so I had to look at him. Then he kissed me." She paused for a moment, the bile rising in her throat as it had every time she thought about that incident.

Taking a breath Annabelle continued. "I'd never been kissed before and thought it the most disgusting thing I had ever experienced. I gagged, and he took it as an insult. He punches when he doesn't like what you do, but he is wise: my face he left alone."

Grace and Rosalind were crying, but Eleanor could not; she just watched her sister, hardly blinking as she absorbed the information.

"He threw me against the door and told me to get out that I wasn't worth his bother. I ran all the way home and retired to my bedchamber. My arms were bruised, but my nightgown covered everything. I was so relieved when you went to the theatre, I thought I would have time to weep in private, so no one would find out. I did try and tell mother something, but she just told me to keep out of his way. I'm not sure if she detected something was amiss or knew what his character was, but she didn't help when I needed her to."

"Then a few days afterwards there was a dinner party he had not been invited to. I don't know if you remember it, Grace; you had retired early, and I'd gone to my bedchamber. I don't know how he got in; the first thing I realised was when I heard the key turn in the lock. That's when the tears of self-pity turned into tears of fear," Annabelle continued. "He was determined to hurt me for humiliating him," she said quietly. "I lost hair, was bitten, punched and slapped until I didn't know where I was. But all the time he was kissing me, forcing his lips on mine and his tongue down my throat. Then he dropped the front of his pants and forced himself on top of me."

"Oh, Good God, no!" Rosalind wailed.

Annabelle smiled a small bitter smile. "He forced himself on me; I bled, but he wasn't satisfied for many hours: he knew we would not be disturbed because of what was going on downstairs. He eventually left, but I couldn't move. Thank God for Lucy." Annabelle would be forever grateful to her loyal maid. "She had come into the room to prepare for morning, and I had screamed out, thinking it was him returned. I nearly terrified her, but she realised at least some of what had happened."

"Lucy took care of everything. She cleaned me, nursed me and wiped my tears for days. I had already started the farce of being ill, so it was easy to continue it. When the bruises and scratches had faded I was able to resume life, although I never thought I would ever feel normal again."

"I wish I had known," Grace said sadly.

This time it was Annabelle's turn to squeeze her sister's hand in comfort. "There was nothing you could have done. I talked everything through with Lucy. I wouldn't have been believed; father thought there was no one better than Mr Wadeson. It would have just been proof he had chosen which sister to marry, so I chose to stay quiet; I could never have married him."

"Of course not!" Rosalind said, anger bubbling inside her like never before.

"I'm sorry I left you Grace," Annabelle said with genuine remorse. "Now I know what risk I was putting you in, but then, all I could think about was escaping."

"There's nothing to worry about; I was fine: he didn't touch me," Grace insisted.

Rosalind had to ask a question. "Annabelle, what did you tell Lord Stannage?"

Annabelle smiled a little. "It nearly cost me my marriage to my darling husband," she started. "Every time he tried to kiss me, all I could see was Mr Wadeson; it made me avoid any close contact with Frederick. Which for Frederick just made him think I was regretting marrying him because of his eyes. I tried to explain that it wasn't, but I couldn't find the right words. It was a horrible situation, but I didn't think I could tell him."

"I'm presuming you did?" Grace asked.

"Yes," Annabelle smiled. "It was harder than telling you; at least I know I have your love, but with him, he could have rejected me and ruined me in the process."

"What did he do?" Eleanor asked.

"He was the angriest I've ever seen him, but it gave him something to fight against. He was very patient and loving and now I know how a husband and wife can love each other, and it is nothing like what that man did to me. Frederick didn't mind that I was not an innocent; he just cared for me and has wiped out some of the memories," Annabelle said with a smile. "I will love him for it until my dying day."

"I knew he was a good man; thankfully he is clearly one of the best," Rosalind said with approval. "Now we have to decide what to do."

"What do you mean?" Annabelle asked in alarm.

"Well, we can't let this go unpunished," Rosalind said firmly. "He may think he has got away with it, but he won't!"

"No!" Annabelle cried out. "Rosalind, I have been through all of this; nothing has changed. Father still thinks the world of him, so he will believe Mr Wadeson over me, and if it comes out, I am ruined and Frederick is even more of a laughing stock. I won't put him through that; he has been through enough. Seeing Mr Wadeson last night was bad enough for him; he says he wants to kill the man for what he did, but he has promised me he will not act on it." Annabelle knew of the ridicule her husband had been through because of his different coloured eyes; she was determined he would not continue to suffer because of her.

"She's right, Rosalind," Grace said. "There is nothing to gain, but we must tell Harry and Peter. We will need their support."

"They will condemn me," Annabelle said quietly.

"They certainly will not!" Grace said indignantly. "We don't need to tell them everything, just enough so they know not to leave Eleanor alone. The more people we have surrounding her, the safer she will be."

"I will still have to marry him," Eleanor said dully. She had listened with horror to her sister's story and now was filled with dread at the thought of being married to such a man. It had seemed like a poor situation before, marrying a man she did not know, but now, for the first time she was filled with fear.

"We will have to try and dissuade Father," Rosalind responded.

"That will make no difference; look how much he listened to you when you didn't want to marry Peter," Eleanor replied realistically. "I may need to disappear."

"Where to?" Rosalind asked, immediately worried.

"I have no idea, but it will have to be somewhere I am sure will be safe," Eleanor replied, her frown betraying the worry the afternoon had created.

Chapter 12

It was a more subdued group that returned to the Hall. They were each engrossed in their own thoughts. Annabelle felt drained and, when they entered the hallway, she excused herself to go for a lie down. She needed to find Frederick; she felt completely safe only when she was near him.

Rosalind led the way into the library; she did not feel like going into one of the rooms that would more likely have someone in them. The disadvantage to a busy house was the places to escape were lessened; although after what they had heard, that would be a distinct advantage over the coming days.

Rosalind and Eleanor sat quietly together, Rosalind holding her sister's hand. Eventually she spoke. "I suggest you have a portmanteau packed and ready in case you need to leave suddenly. I can help you go through your clothes and mine; thankfully we are of a similar height. I will also have Peter give you an amount of money that will provide for you for quite a while. We just need to think where you are to go."

"Are you sending me away now?" Eleanor asked surprised. Rosalind was always being teased for wanting her sisters to be nearby.

"We can't keep you safe here," Rosalind said sadly. "I thought of everything we could try and do, but he could still get to you. He may have forced himself on one of my sister's, but he is certainly not going to force himself on another!"

"Where am I to go? Should I return to Bath?" Eleanor asked.

"No, I thought of that, but father would check there first. You need to be somewhere harder to find, but I just can't think of anywhere yet. I will speak to Peter about it. Don't mention it to Grace and Annabelle. I don't like having secrets, but the fewer people know, the better."

"I'm scared, Rosalind," Eleanor said. It was true; she always acted older than her years, but what she had heard that afternoon had been beyond her comprehension, especially when the realisation dawned that she was the man's next victim.

Rosalind wrapped Eleanor in her arms. "Don't worry; we will get you through this."

They stayed together, holding and being held in a way they had not done for years. Eleanor felt comfortable snuggled against Rosalind; her eldest sister really had been a mother to her. After a while Eleanor noticed Rosalind was going stiff every few minutes, and she sat up to look at her sister.

"Rosalind, what is it?" Eleanor asked, noticing her sister's pale face.

Just at that moment the door opened, and Joseph entered the room. He saw the two ladies and offered his apologies for intruding and was in the process of withdrawing, but Rosalind called out to him, making him pause.

"Mr Heaton, please come in!" Rosalind said, the sharpness in her voice bringing Joseph into the room without question. "I need your help. It seems that my child is arriving a little before it was expected."

"I shall seek help," Joseph said, moving once more to the door.

"No!" Rosalind almost shouted. Joseph paused once more and turned to face Rosalind. He noticed her face was taut with pain, but she was staring at him in fear. "Mr Heaton, my sister needs a protector. Please do not ask me to explain, but you are an intelligent man. I am speaking not as an hysterical female, but as one who is terrified for the safety of a beloved sister. Am I making myself clear?"

"You need my help," Joseph said, not really understanding but accepting Rosalind's words all the same.

"My baby's timing is poor at best as it means I cannot protect Eleanor. The house will be sent into chaos once we go through those doors, so before we do, I need your word that, whatever happens, you will not leave my sister alone."

"I will not," Joseph promised.

"You do not realise how serious I am being. She is only to be left when in the company of another of our sisters, my husband, Harry, or Frederick, no one else. Do I make myself clear? Absolutely no one else!"

"You have my word," Joseph said calmly. "Miss Johnson, please help me support your sister to her chamber; I think if we don't move soon, her child will be born in the library."

Eleanor helped as much as she could, but in reality Joseph took Rosalind's weight and supported her up the stairs. The ever efficient Bryant had staff scurrying within seconds of the three persons leaving the library. Joseph and Eleanor were dismissed once they had helped Rosalind through her bedchamber door. The last words they heard from Rosalind were, "Don't forget you've given your word, Mr Heaton."

Joseph looked at Eleanor when they were in the hallway. "I suggest we go for that phaeton ride we never had the opportunity to do in Bath."

"But I should be near Rosalind...." Eleanor started.

"No one will try and separate us if we are out of the building," Joseph reasoned. He needed to get Eleanor away; whatever was going on had affected her deeply. She looked terrified, and he knew it was not purely to do with her sister's confinement. Something was very wrong and, even without his promise to Rosalind, he would defend Eleanor, to the death if needed.

Eleanor nodded, and the pair took it in turns to visit their bedchambers to retrieve bonnets and hats. Joseph had a message sent to the stables and, within a short space of time, they were travelling at speed through the parkland.

The pace did not slow until they were far removed from the house. Joseph had no clear idea where he was going, so he just let the horses burn off their first burst of energy, travelling down the main roadways. After fifteen minutes the horses settled into a steadier pace, and Joseph looked at Eleanor. She had remained still, her pensive expression never veering from the direction they were travelling.

Joseph's chest was tight; there was obviously something very wrong, but he was not sure how much she would confide in him.

"Is there anywhere you wish us to travel to?" Joseph asked breaking the silence.

Eleanor looked at him with a small smile. "We are both strangers to the area; I'm afraid I don't know of any of the local attractions."

"We shall have to be explorers then and discover the darkest secrets Lancashire has to offer together," Joseph said with a smile. Eleanor smiled in response but did not speak. Joseph decided his timing might not be perfect, but he wanted to try and clear the air between them. If he was to be her protector from goodness knew what, it would be easier if she trusted him.

"I had planned we would share a phaeton on that day in Bath," he said quietly. Eleanor looked at him warily, so he continued carefully. "I was going to tell you how much I thought about you when you were not near me."

Eleanor looked away. "Please don't," she said; if he were playing some game with her, she could not bear it. There were too many emotions coursing through her body already.

Joseph stopped the phaeton, securing the reins before turning towards Eleanor. "Please let me explain. I hate to think I hurt you, of all people." Eleanor looked at him, the pain showing clearly in her eyes. "Oh, Eleanor, you do not know how I curse myself for that stupid conversation. I detest myself to think it has caused you so much pain."

Eleanor had not given him permission to use her given name, but she made no comment on his presumption; there were more important things to sort out. "Did you mean what you said?"

Joseph was in turmoil. He should lie and work to gain her favour, but he could not. He had to be truthful no matter the cost. "Do you know when I look back, I hardly recognise myself? Yes, I'm ashamed to say when I said them I was being an arrogant fool, and I did mean them."

Eleanor closed her eyes for the briefest of moments; Joseph felt as if he had struck her, but continued on. "I'm not excusing my words, but please listen. I have one of the highest titles in the country and the wealth to match it. People respond to you in a certain way when you are so privileged; I was surrounded by people who thought that everything I said was funny and every opinion I had was valid. It is easy as a man without some reality to keep him grounded to become arrogant, very arrogant in my case."

"You won't get any arguments from me with regards to that," Eleanor said quietly, but she smiled, which was the beacon of hope Joseph was waiting for.

Joseph continued, responding to her smile with one of his own. "I was arrogant, and I can't guarantee I am completely reformed; I'm sure there will be lapses, but those idiotic words were said by a man I no longer know."

"You regret them so much they have changed you?" Eleanor asked surprised.

"No, although I do regret saying them," Joseph explained. "When I arrived in Bath, it was with the intention of hiding who I was to try and have some semblance of normality, but I went with the wrong attitude. I was still being arrogant by presuming I could play with Lady Lydia's affections and the affections of her friend. So, instead of people using me, I was intent on using others."

Eleanor could see it was costing Joseph to speak so frankly, but it was clear he was telling the truth. His frown and the way he brushed his hand over his face in frustration showed a little of his inner turmoil.

"The only thing I hadn't anticipated was meeting you," Joseph said with a small smile. "It was clear from the start you didn't care who I was: you were so accepting and open; but I somehow knew I wouldn't need a title and a large fortune to gain favour with you, but I wanted to earn your respect. You were so matter-of-fact about what your father was and his plans for his family that I couldn't help but admire you."

"There was no point being anything but realistic about my lot in life," Eleanor said.

"But the more I got to know you, the more I needed to be near you. I went to bed every night thinking about you and woke up every morning wanting to be with you. I was wrong to kiss you, but I will always be glad I did." The blush that spread across Eleanor's cheeks at his words encouraged Joseph. "I want to do it again."

"We are in a public place!" Eleanor exclaimed.

"That wasn't a no!" Joseph said, surprising Eleanor with the speed he jumped onto the ground and moved around to her side. He reached up his arms and lifted her down as if she weighed very little. Moving into the trees that lined the road, he threw his stove top hat onto the ground and turned to Eleanor.

Her heart was pounding as Joseph slowly undid the ribbons that tied her bonnet and then threw the straw contraption onto the ground next to the stove top. Eleanor's face was cupped in strong hands but held gently.

"Oh, Eleanor, you don't realise how much I have missed you. It has been torture without you nearby," Joseph whispered before kissing her.

Eleanor did not resist; she did not want to resist. The emotion of the day added to her feelings of missing Joseph and made her lean into him with a sigh. Joseph felt his legs weaken at the sound.

"I only want to make you happy," he whispered. "I'm sorry I hurt you."

"It doesn't matter anymore," Eleanor whispered in return. She was not sure what her future held; all she knew was he was here with her now, and he wanted her.

Joseph had no idea how long they spent together, hidden, enjoying the kisses that should have already been shared and would have been but for his stupidity. Eventually, he pulled away from her lips but held her close. "I suppose we should continue with our ride," he said, nibbling her ear.

Eleanor laughed quietly at the tickling sensation. "I suppose we should or do you think we should return to Rosalind?"

"I believe these things can take some time; I don't think there is any hurry," Joseph said. He was no expert, but in the snippets of conversation he had overheard, childbirth seemed to take hours.

"We can continue our journey then," Eleanor said, not really wishing to return too soon. Joseph walked, holding Eleanor's hand and bent to retrieve her bonnet. He placed it on her head and tied the ribbon securely under her chin, kissing her when he had finished.

"I suggest you don't remove your bonnet until you are in the privacy of your room. The state of your hair will raise some questions," Joseph said.

Eleanor looked mortified, "I must look a state!"

Joseph held her hands and looked intensely into her eyes. "Your hair is ruffled, your lips are bruised, your cheeks are flushed and your eyes look like the depths of the ocean. I have never seen you look so beautiful." He let go of Eleanor's hands and took hold of her face, gently moving her to face him once more; she had turned away at his words.

When he forced her to look into his eyes, he spoke, his voice gruff. "To me, you are the most beautiful woman I have ever met. Yes, I admit you haven't got the blonde hair and blue eyes Lady Lydia has and a thousand like her, but you have something different. When you laugh, your eyes sparkle as I've never seen before; when you look at me I feel you are looking into my soul. I watch your every expression and my stomach and chest respond to them. You are more than a classic beauty, Eleanor; never react negatively to a compliment when in my company, or I may have to react rashly."

"Why, what will you do?" Eleanor asked alarmed.

"No matter who is in company with us, I will kiss you; do you understand? If I hear one derogatory comment from that pretty mouth of yours about your looks, I will kiss you. I give you my word," Joseph said roughly.

Eleanor smiled. "I may just have to say I am ugly a few times to test it out."

Joseph laughed and kissed her before lifting her up to the phaeton. "We are going to be the talk of the locality."

They continued onwards, Joseph controlling the horses with one hand, while holding Eleanor's with his other. Occasionally he would bring her hand to his lips and kiss it gently. After a while Joseph turned to Eleanor with a frown. "Why does Rosalind think you are in some sort of danger?"

Eleanor stiffened, the afternoon had been going so well; she had been able to put the details of the morning behind her, but she had been aware it was a temporary respite. She pondered for a few moments before answering. She was not sure how much of Annabelle's story to tell; the more people who knew, the more likely the news would spread, and the news would ruin the family.

"My sisters know enough of Mr Wadeson's character to be convinced he can behave outside the boundaries of propriety," she started carefully. "My father has decided I am to marry him, and they believe that knowledge may encourage him to seek me out while they're trying think of a reason I should not marry him."

Joseph squeezed Eleanor's hand unconsciously, and it was only when she winced he was brought to his senses. "I'm sorry," he apologised. "Will they think of a reason that will convince your father to change his mind?" he asked abruptly.

"No, I don't believe they will," Eleanor said resignedly. "He has never listened to any of us, and he is determined his business will remain in the family. There is only myself remaining to fulfil that wish, and he thinks there is no one better than Mr Wadeson."

"Let me speak to him," Joseph said with a growl, a plan immediately springing to mind, but he did not wish to mention anything to Eleanor. To offer for her without the approval of her father would be cruel, although he was determined to do everything he could to persuade Mr Johnson.

"Joseph, I'm afraid," Eleanor said, finally voicing the feeling she had felt since Annabelle started to tell her story.

Joseph looked at her. "Don't be; I'm here."

Eleanor would cling to those words for the hours and days to come.

Chapter 13

They eventually returned when the light was fading to find that Rosalind was still not through her ordeal. Everyone was gathered in the drawing room apart from Mr Wadeson, who had sensed there was some animosity towards him that had not been there on the first evening. He excused himself and returned to his bedchamber.

Annabelle looked as if she had been crying, and Frederick looked like thunder, but he sat close to Annabelle, his arm around her in a defiant act of support. Eleanor was more worried about her eldest sister than she was about herself. She had Joseph with her, and she knew without doubt he would protect her.

Peter was as nervous as all previous expectant fathers before him had been. He was pacing the room, not concentrating on anything going on around him. After a while Mr Johnson tired of the company and removed himself to the library. Joseph approached Frederick and indicated he wished to speak to him. Frederick reluctantly left Annabelle's side, but he followed Joseph to the window.

"I need to speak to Mr Johnson, but I don't wish for Eleanor to be in a position where she is unaccompanied if she needs to leave the room," Joseph said quietly.

"Don't worry; I won't be leaving either Annabelle or Eleanor alone for a moment," Frederick said gritting his teeth. "I would hang for killing the low life, if it didn't mean leaving Annabelle."

"I don't know why there is the need to act in this way, but I'm presuming it is vital that we do," Joseph said. "I was asked to not leave Eleanor alone unless she was with her sisters or their husbands, but there was no mention of her father or Mr Wadeson." He was hoping Frederick would tell him more of what he wanted to know.

"It's Wadeson, but the father seems to hold him in the highest regard, so I wouldn't trust him to protect any of them," Frederick ground out.

Joseph frowned; he had thought only Eleanor was at risk from something, but from Frederick's words, it seemed all the sisters were at risk. He did not like not knowing what was going on; he was a man always fully in control, but at least now he had a little more information to work with.

"I shall return shortly," he said before leaving the room.

Eleanor followed Joseph's movements with a frown on her face. She felt a moment of panic when he left the room, but Frederick walked behind her and patted her gently on her shoulder in reassurance before sitting down next to Annabelle. The drawing room door opened once more to allow access for Grace and Harry to enter the room.

"Any news?" Grace asked the room at large.

"Nothing. I don't understand what's taking so long," Peter growled, running his hand through his hair in frustration.

Grace approached him and slipped her arm through his. "She is strong. She will be well."

"I hope so Grace; I couldn't bear anything to happen to her. I just couldn't," Peter said quietly, his voice cracking.

"I know," Grace said, resting her head on his arm in silent reassurance.

*

Joseph entered the library, and Mr Johnson looked up. "Any news?" the older man asked.

"No," Joseph replied. "I would like to speak with you in private."

Mr Johnson indicated Joseph should take the seat opposite him. Joseph was slightly amused Mr Johnson was not reading for pleasure but had business papers he was reading. The man was evidently always working.

"It's about your youngest daughter," Joseph said wanting to come straight to the point.

"Oh?" Mr Johnson said, moving the papers to one side.

"I wish to ask for your permission to marry her," Joseph continued.

"Oh, you do, do you? I've some bad news for you; she is already betrothed," Mr Johnson, replied.

"I've been told you wished all of your daughters to marry a title. I realise that one hasn't, but I am a Duke with wealth that is beyond all I could spend in a lifetime," Joseph said. He would not normally have been so crass, but he wanted to put forward the best case possible. "I would care for your daughter so a dowry is irrelevant. You could put it in trust for any children we might have who will all be titled. In the meantime I would like to explore the possibility of going into business with you."

Mr Johnson looked at Joseph with interest. "You want to go into business with me? You, a Duke?"

Joseph nodded. "Yes. I know you wish the family business to stay in the family; this way I would be giving you the option of giving your youngest daughter the title and the business."

Mr Johnson sat quietly, assessing Joseph. He had detected some interest towards his daughter; he was not a fool, but he had been surprised at the offer of going into business.

Joseph waited patiently. He met Mr Johnson's stare; he was not afraid of the man: in fact, he did not have a high opinion of him at all. Both from the information Eleanor had said in Bath and now the new situation they were facing.

Eventually Mr Johnson leaned back in the chair. "Your offer is an interesting one, but I've already made up my mind; Eleanor is to marry Wadeson."

Joseph fought to keep the bile from rising in his throat at the thought of Mr Wadeson and Eleanor together. He suddenly realised how much he needed Eleanor to be his. He had known he thought highly of her, but when it was clear she might be lost to him, it struck him that he was completely in love with her, and he could not lose her a second time.

"This will sound boastful, but she will have better connections with me than with anyone else," Joseph responded.

Mr Johnson laughed. "You'll be telling me next you have an excellent business mind."

"I've got enough of one that my fortune has grown since I've held the title," Joseph responded. "I'm not trying to say I have the knowledge to take over your business now, but I imagine you don't wish to step down just yet. I can learn while you are still at the helm; it will be a smoother transition that way."

Mr Johnson sighed. "When I started on the scheme to marry the girls to men with titles, I did not think about my feelings in the matter. I don't wish for what I have built up to be lost, and that would be the same with you. You want to give me your commitment, but six months into learning about the business, you could lose interest when it is the hunting season or some such nonsense. I want steadiness."

Joseph bristled at his words but kept his tone even. "I could accuse you of not being steady, changing your mind about your aims when there is the opportunity to complete what you started."

Mr Johnson narrowed his eyes. "In business, you have to react to the market needs; that way, you will stay in business when others flounder. I am reacting in the best way of providing for my daughter's future and seeing my business profit. Wadeson is the man to do that."

"But what if your daughter does not wish it?" Joseph asked.

"The day I listen to my daughters will be the day they put me in the ground! My decisions have been proven to be correct; if you would have heard the arguments Rosalind put up before marrying her Duke, you would understand my sentiments. She swore she would never be happy, yet she is. My judgement is sound, and I stick to my decision: Wadeson is to marry Eleanor."

"Can I do nothing to change your mind?" Joseph said, a note of desperation seeping into his voice.

"No. And don't think that finding you both in a compromising position will change my mind; Wadeson wouldn't be deterred by that. He wants the business; Eleanor is just the added benefit," Mr Johnson finished. It was clear he thought the interview was over as he picked up his papers and started to read.

Joseph stood up, anger rushing through every fibre of his being. "I am convinced your judgement is flawed when you can't see the flaws that are so blatant to anyone else coming into contact with the man, but I hope when I have daughters I never consider treating them in such a callous way. You don't deserve the family you have, Mr Johnson."

Any reply was prevented from being uttered by the entrance of Grace. "Rosalind has had a boy," she announced proudly.

*

Eleanor was locked in her bedchamber. The door to her dressing room was also locked. Annabelle and Frederick had escorted her to her rooms after everyone had seen Rosalind. Her sister was exhausted but smiling when the three sisters had entered.

The baby had been in his mother's arms, all scrunched and red, but fast asleep. Rosalind held out her hands to her sisters, and they gathered around, kissing her and congratulating her. Peter remained in the background, allowing the important meeting but not willing to leave his wife for a moment.

Rosalind turned to Eleanor. "Are you well?" she asked urgently.

"I am; Mr Heaton has hardly left my side," she said reassuringly.

"We will not let her be alone," Annabelle assured Rosalind. "You mustn't worry."

"I will always worry about my babies," Rosalind said with a tired smile.

"Rest. That is what you are to do now," Grace said with firmness. "We shall see you tomorrow."

It had been easy to be brave when people surrounded you, Eleanor thought with a shudder. Now locked in her room, she did not feel so brave. Annabelle had suggested she have her maid sleep in her dressing room, but Eleanor refused.

"There is no need to have more people involved than is absolutely necessary," Eleanor said.

"I want you to be safe," Annabelle had replied.

"I will be locked in here. Knock in the morning, and we can go to breakfast together," Eleanor said. Her maid would knock on the door when she found it locked, so until then Eleanor would not open the door.

As she sat in her bed, her knees huddled under her chin she did not feel as confident as she had. She wanted Joseph's protection but could not seek him out at night. There were limits to what he could do.

She was startled from her thoughts by the door knob turning. Eleanor stilled, listening for any sound she would recognise. Another try at the door brought a gentle knocking.

She moved off the bed and quietly padded to the door. It could be Joseph she reasoned. She placed her ear near the key-hole to see if she could distinguish any noise, but whoever was on the other side was being equally as quiet. Eventually she heard footsteps walk down the hallway that were obviously a man's heavy thread. Sinking to the floor, shaking, Eleanor realised it could only be one person. She felt a chill creep over her; she could not marry that man.

Chapter 14

Mrs Adams was delighted Rosalind was safe after the birth of baby Peter James but was sorry Rosalind would miss Stuart's wedding. Preparations had been made and finally the day arrived. Much of the locality were invited; Peter had offered the use of the ballroom to host the wedding breakfast: it was to be a day of celebration.

Frances was accompanied by Annabelle as her matron of honour. If it had not been for Annabelle's invitation she would probably never have had the opportunity to rekindle feelings for her future husband that she had spent so long repressing.

Annabelle helped fasten a ribbon around Frances's neck that held a topaz droplet. The ribbon matched the cream of the gown she wore, contrasting with the rich colour of the jewel. Her hair was tied with topaz coloured clips, and Harry had supplied flowers for Grace to make into a wedding bouquet. He had supplied cream and blue irises and blue primula that Grace used around the edge of the bouquet of irises that complemented the topaz for a truly stunning effect.

Frances looked at Annabelle through her looking glass. "I love him; is it normal to feel so nervous?"

Annabelle laughed and moved around to face her friend. "It is, but you have absolutely nothing to worry about. He is besotted with you and a decent man into the bargain. What more could you ask for?"

"I'm afraid of letting him down; he is so well educated and travelled. What if he should tire of me?" Frances asked worriedly. The doubts had dogged her from the start and, although Stuart and Mrs Adams had reassured her, on a day so full of emotion her insecurities were bound to return.

"I'm no expert in marriage," Annabelle started, referring to her own shaky start. "But I can see when somebody truly cares for someone else. Mr Adams dotes on you; it is clear in his every mannerism towards you. If I hadn't found my own dear Frederick, I would be quite jealous!" she laughed.

"I cannot believe I have been so lucky," Frances said quietly.

"Well, I can; you are a lovely person and a true friend who happens to look beautiful. Come, we have a wedding to go to," Annabelle said, linking her friend's arm and walking down the stairs to join the other members of Frances's family.

The ceremony went without a hitch, although there was quite a stir when people saw Mrs Adams wipe her eye as her son said his vows. Whispering was to be heard, but was soon put paid when Mrs Adams turned to look at the gathered throng with a glare. Only Frances and Annabelle noticed the smile that replaced the glare once she was facing the front of the church.

A hundred people gathered in the ballroom of Sudworth Hall to celebrate the wedding. Mr Johnson and Mr Wadeson were absent, Mr Johnson using the day to progress his business enquiries as he did not know the bride and groom. It meant everyone connected to the Johnson women could relax, knowing there was no threat to Eleanor's safety.

Joseph had watched Eleanor throughout the ceremony. For that day he did not need to feel he was protecting her but could look at her as the object of his heart. She had looked pensive for the last few days, and he could understand completely, but today she looked more relaxed.

She was dressed in a peach dress, which set off her hair colour to perfection. The style was plain but elegant with a short train at the back of the dress. It emphasised her height, and she looked elegant, perfect to be his duchess, he mused to himself. He had no idea how he was going to change Mr Johnson's mind, but he knew he would have to try again.

Eleanor looked over at Joseph, knowing he was watching her. It made something uncurl in her stomach every time she looked up and saw his smiling eyes seeking hers. For the first time in her life she felt connected to someone other than her sisters. She had not been kissed by him since the day baby Peter had been born, and she longed to feel his arms around her again.

She decided it was safe enough to risk doing something that, although it would cause her to blush, would be worth the embarrassment. She carefully indicated Joseph should follow her and, when it would not be noticed by anyone else, she left the ballroom. Walking through the hallway, she was relieved there were no footmen present; it would not do to have her actions observed. She waited at the door to the library until

Joseph walked through the door from the ballroom, then she entered the library her cheeks red, but her heart pounding in anticipation.

Joseph smiled to himself as he followed Eleanor. He leaned against the library door, once he entered and turned the key in the lock. "Do you want to speak to me, Miss Johnson?" he said feigning ignorance.

"I wondered if you required some wine," Eleanor said, picking up a glass she had poured and taking a sip, watching Joseph over the rim.

Joseph groaned and pushed off the door. He pulled the glass from Eleanor's grasp and pulled her towards him. "We shouldn't; we could be caught," he muttered before crushing his lips to hers. The taste of wine reminded him of the first time they had kissed, and he wrapped her close, his arms drawing her fully against him.

Eleanor's arms snaked around his neck and held his head tight against her lips. She didn't know if it was the pressure of the last few days or if her feelings were increasing naturally, but she returned his kisses as passionately as he gave them.

Joseph picked her up and turned her against the wall. He needed the support of something solid, before he melted to the floor; her responses were beyond what he had hoped for, and it was intoxicating.

He moved his hands, exploring her body, and she did not stop him, her gasps of pleasure being swallowed by his kisses. He pulled his mouth away from hers. "Eleanor, I want you as I have never wanted anyone or anything in my life before. I can't think straight."

"You know what my future is to be, but I want you too," Eleanor said with a blush. It was true: she loved the man; he held her with passion but as if she was precious.

Joseph groaned. "Eleanor, I fight my demons every night when I retire. All I want to do is to join you in your bedchamber and make you mine."

Eleanor took a sharp breath. "Was it you the other night?" she asked.

"When?" Joseph asked, his hands still.

"A few nights ago, when Rosalind had the baby; I had locked my door. Did you try to get in?"

"No. I said I fought my urges; I would never carry them through," Joseph said, but his tone was like steel. All thoughts of kisses stopped.

"Oh," Eleanor said, realising her words had spoiled the mood.

"I will kill him!" Joseph said, walking away from her.

"No!" Eleanor exclaimed. "I'm not sure it was him; look how I thought it was you. I could be wrong."

Joseph looked at her. "We both know you aren't," he said shortly.

Eleanor's arms wrapped around herself. "I'm sorry; I shouldn't have mentioned anything."

Joseph walked back to her and took her chin between his thumb and finger. "Yes, you should," he said quietly. "I'm only frustrated because, for whatever reason, that man has the upper hand; he is promised to you, and there isn't a damn thing I can do about it."

"You could compromise me," Eleanor said, embarrassed at her words but saying them anyway.

Joseph smiled at the colour of her cheeks. "I already thought of that, but so had your father. He said even if I did, Wadeson would still marry you. He is determined to go ahead with his plan."

Eleanor felt panicked and afraid at the situation being forced on her. She felt out of control, but then something struck her. It would mean her behaving like a wanton doxy, but she would at least achieve what she wanted out of it. She looked at Joseph, her determined stare taking him by surprise.

"What are you thinking?" Joseph asked, alert at the change in Eleanor.

"We want each other and, even if I am compromised, I am to marry that frightful man," Eleanor said.

"Yes?" Joseph said, thinking he knew where the conversation was leading.

"I would like you to visit my chamber tonight," Eleanor asked, for once not blushing.

"Do you realise what you are saying?" Joseph said, his mouth drying with the thoughts of what he was being offered.

"Yes. For once in my life I am going to take control of what is happening to me," Eleanor said firmly. "If I am to marry someone I will never care for, I am going to spend the nights before that wedding with the man I do want. My father can force me into a farce of a marriage, but my body is my own to give to whom I wish."

"Eleanor, don't make that decision lightly," Joseph said quietly. "Once it is made, there will be no going back. Your husband will find out on your wedding night he is not your first."

"If he is not concerned whether I am an innocent or not, which he clearly is not if my father's words are true, then why should I give to him the one thing that, if I give to you, will link us together always?" Eleanor asked seriously.

"I will always be linked to you even if you don't give me your innocence," Joseph said. "Eleanor, I don't know if I could have you once and then be able to walk away. I'm struggling with accepting that you belong to another after sharing only kisses with you."

"It won't be the once," Eleanor said crossing to him. She wrapped her arms around his neck and looked into his eyes. She could see the turmoil within him. "I want you to share every night with me until I marry. I want to feel what it is like to be loved for who I am by someone who thinks I'm beautiful."

"And what about after you are married?" Joseph said, not sure that he could ever give her up.

"I don't know how at this moment, but I need you to be in my life," Eleanor said seriously.

"Good God, Eleanor! You are torturing me," Joseph whispered, his eyes bright. "Are you sure? It wasn't so long ago you would have cursed me to the devil."

"A lot has changed since then; I've learned how harsh the world can be, and I want to feel loved," Eleanor said quietly.

"I do love you; you know that, don't you?" Joseph was urgent. He needed her to know he was not just using her.

"I know," Eleanor said before kissing him gently.

Joseph returned the kiss but then held her against him. What they had spoken about went beyond kisses. He had never before told anyone he loved them. The ever confident Duke was out of his depth for the first time in his life, and it terrified him.

They arranged that a particular knock would identify Joseph from anyone else wishing to gain access and then they returned to the celebrations. Their absence had been long, but neither was too concerned; they were not the focus of attention and doubted anyone would have noticed their absence.

*

Eleanor had not been able to settle in any seat since getting into her nightwear and dismissing her maid. She could not sit on her bed; it suddenly felt an overwhelming place to be. She was sure she wanted to be with Joseph, but that did not make the night any less daunting.

The specified knock came, and she moved to the door. "Joseph?" she whispered, still wary of unlocking the door.

"Yes, it's me," Joseph whispered into the door.

Eleanor quickly unlocked the door and allowed him entry, closing and locking the door behind him. "Did you see anyone?" Eleanor asked. She did not wish her sisters to think she was a loose woman; their good opinion she never wanted to lose, and she was not sure if they would understand her sentiments.

"No, don't worry," Joseph said with a smile of reassurance. "Come here," he said, drawing her into his arms. He held her for a moment or two, concerned that she was shaking slightly.

Eventually when she settled into his arms, he kissed the top of her head. "You do not have to do anything you do not wish to. I will not think any less of you if you have changed your mind."

Eleanor stood straight and looked at Joseph. He was all love and concern; she smiled. "I have changed my mind a hundred times since this afternoon, but not for the reasons you will presume. I want it to happen; I am just a little afraid. I suppose it is only natural," she said, trying to seem unconcerned.

Joseph leaned forward and kissed her gently. "I imagine it is, but you are fortunate in that you have got such a fine specimen before you; it can only guarantee you shall have a night full of enjoyment!"

Joseph's words had the desired effect. Eleanor laughed and looked at him archly, "Oh, yes? I hope I'm not to be disappointed, Your Grace!"

She used his title to tease, but Joseph smiled wolfishly. "I like your being respectful; it does something wicked in my stomach, but I think I want you to call me Joseph from now on."

"Not Joe?" Eleanor asked, stroking his face. "Not my Joe?"

Joseph moaned. "I think I have been yours since the moment I met you."

He stopped talking and kissed her fully, all thoughts of relaxing her gone as his passion took over. He would never lose so much control he would forget her needs and that it was her first time, but he was determined she would enjoy the experience as much as he.

*

Many hours later Eleanor lay snuggled up to Joseph's side, his arm around her, drawing her close to him. Her hand played with the hairs on his chest, as he dozed. She had already been asleep, exhausted but happy. He had been perfect with her, loving her gently and keeping his promise; it would be a night she would never forget.

Waking up being held by Joseph had been almost as perfect as the lovemaking; she felt secure and happy, and she did not want anything to change that.

He had opened the curtains slightly, so they could watch the dawn together. He was determined to fill their time alone with as many memories as would see them through the following months. He could not think about that time at the moment; he did not wish to spoil what little time they had together, but life was going to be very dark in the future.

She had been everything he had hoped for. She was innocent, but not lacking in passion; he had guided her and encouraged her until he felt he would never want to make love to anyone else ever again, he was so drained. As he woke from his doze, he realised, with Eleanor at his side, he would always want to make love.

He pushed Eleanor on her back. She laughed up at him as he kissed her. "You are too tempting to leave alone," he whispered nibbling her jaw.

"More?" she asked weakly.

Joseph looked at her with a wicked grin. "Are you saying I have worn out my darling Eleanor?"

"Maybe," she said with a shy smile. "Maybe not."

"That's the type of answer I like," Joseph replied before showing her just how ready for more he was.

When they heard movement in the household, the staff preparing the house for life once more, Joseph moved. "It is time I left," he said reluctantly. "You may have been compromised, but I don't want the world to know about it."

Eleanor sighed; she knew he was right. She placed her hand on his back, as he sat on the edge of her bed, reaching for his clothing. "Will you come back?"

Joseph paused and looked over his shoulder at her. "I will come back as long as you wish me to. I love you Eleanor; what we are doing goes against everything I've always believed in, but I can't keep away from you; I would do anything to make you happy."

"Thank you," she said. She pulled the covers over herself and watched as he readied himself. When he was dressed, she stepped out of the bed, pulling her nightgown over her shoulders. She had to lock the door after he left. They could not be complacent.

Joseph kissed her gently. "If I had my way, you would never wear a nightgown again."

Eleanor blushed, which was foolish after what they had shared, but she was not the confident siren she wanted to be if things could work out differently.

Joseph smiled and moved towards the door. "Make sure you lock it behind me, and remember I love you," he said, and with one final kiss, he was gone.

Eleanor did as instructed and then returned to bed. It felt lonely without him, but she could still detect his scent on the bedcovers and eventually fell into an exhausted sleep.

Chapter 15

Mr Wadeson and Eleanor's father joined the family group after morning visits had taken place. Rosalind was still confined to her bedchamber, so Annabelle had taken over the role of lady of the house. It was expected that now Frances and Stuart had married, things would return to normal. Mrs Adams had joined Annabelle and Eleanor for morning visits, still enjoying the amount of chatter focused around her son. Grace always joined the ladies after morning visits; she was as uncomfortable as Annie was, so the two usually entered the room together.

It was unusual to be joined by men at that point, so the women were immediately on the alert. Mrs Adams continued eating her cake, outwardly seeming not to notice the atmosphere had tensed, but in reality watching every movement and noting every word said.

Mr Johnson opened the conversation. "I suppose you want to marry here with your sisters present?" he asked Eleanor.

"Yes," Eleanor replied, all colour draining from her face.

"I thought so; sentimental nonsense, but there seems no point in delaying further. The wedding will take place the day after Rosalind's confinement ends, so seven days from now."

Annabelle and Grace looked horrified, their eyes turned towards Eleanor, but she kept her poise, only her lack of colour betraying her feelings. "I shall start to prepare my trousseau. Where are we to live after we are married?" she asked her father rather than Mr Wadeson.

"Wadeson has a house of his own that will do for now. We'll have a bigger one built near our home. I want him close at hand," Mr Johnson said.

"Obviously," Eleanor responded.

Annie chimed in. "Eleanor, I was Annabelle's and Grace's bridesmaid. Can I be yours?"

Eleanor smiled at the innocence of the girl. Even if she knew the full particulars, she would not understand. "Of course, Annie; it wouldn't be the same without you."

"Good, that is all settled then. We'll be in Preston for the rest of the day. Another few days, and the business will be concluded," Mr Johnson said, rising. "It will have been a productive trip after all."

The group were silent for a few moments after the two gentlemen left. Annie, as always was quick to pick up on a change of atmosphere; she turned to Eleanor. "Why aren't you happy, Eleanor?" she asked, as direct as ever.

Eleanor smiled. "I am very happy you will be my bridesmaid," she said quickly. "Would you like to think of what dress you would like to wear?"

"Oh yes!" Annie said and chatted away, describing her other bridesmaid dresses as if they had not been seen by the others in the room.

Annie's chatter was enough to bring the other sisters out of their own private thoughts and continue their day even though they had received the news that one of them was going to be condemned to a life of violence and cruelty.

Later, Annabelle and Eleanor visited Rosalind as they did every day. They sat talking about everything and anything, until Annabelle could not stand it any longer and told Rosalind of the developments that had taken place.

Rosalind paled as they all had. The realisation the event was to take place brought home how precarious Eleanor's situation was. "We have to do something!" Rosalind said angrily. "We can't just sit back and watch you be offered up as some sort of sacrifice."

"I'm not just sitting back and accepting it," Eleanor said, blushing at the thought of what she had done while the rest of the house was sleeping. "But I am not in a position to do much. I have decided I will go through with the marriage. I will hopefully be able to spend many months visiting the three of you, so I will have some respite."

"Eleanor, you don't understand," Rosalind tried not to scare Eleanor, but at the same time she wanted to make her understand what she was facing. "What happens between a man and a woman is wonderful, but if it is done with cruelty...." Rosalind said, words failing her.

"I do understand," Eleanor said defensively. "More than you know," she continued. "I have made my decision. It's the only way I can accept my lot. I realised once Grace was married that I was destined to marry Mr

Wadeson; the information Annabelle supplied has enabled me to prepare for what I know without doubt will be an unhappy marriage. I must be allowed to get through it the best I can."

"It's not fair!" Rosalind snapped.

"No and neither was marrying you off to Peter, but you love him. I'm not expecting that to happen, but who knows? Mr Wadeson may be completely indifferent to me and leave me alone. He will, after all, have the business once he is married to me," Eleanor said with false brightness.

None of the sisters were convinced, but there was nothing any of them could do. Even as married women, they did not hold any power over their father any more than they had when they were single.

Rosalind sent for Annabelle later in the afternoon. She came straight to the point when Annabelle entered the room. "We need to think of somewhere we can send Eleanor. I will not accept she has to be married to Mr Wadeson."

"Where can she go that will not mean as soon as she is discovered, she will be forced to marry him? You know father will not give up easily," Annabelle asked.

"I've been thinking since you left, and I think I've found a solution. Now that Isabella's claim to the Dukedom has come to nothing, she is going to return to Italy. She no longer visits the hall, staying in the Dower house or with her friends, no doubt going over and over how we have done her wrong," Rosalind said. "She is to return to Italy soon. If Peter spoke to her, I know she would take Eleanor with her for a price. She will do anything to obtain more money from us. We could send Eleanor enough money to set herself up in a small establishment in Italy."

"Rosalind, I understand why you are thinking it, but your idea is flawed," Annabelle said gently. "She would never be able to return to England or us for fear father would find her. Can you honestly say you believe any of us would be able to cope with that, let alone Eleanor? She needs her sisters, as we all do. In some ways it would be a worse fate than what she is facing."

"How can you say that after what he did to you?" Rosalind cried.

"I know it must seem strange, but you are forgetting what we mean to each other. We will all be able to support Eleanor. I will certainly be travelling to stay with her, and I know Frederick will accompany me, even though he hates the man. He will do it to support Eleanor. I know it sounds foolish, but she should be allowed to make her own decision in this."

"I am still going to tell her about my plan," Rosalind insisted. "If she decides against it, at least she will have considered it."

"If it will make you think you have done all you can, make the offer, but she will refuse it."

Annabelle was proved to be correct in her judgement of her sister. Eleanor did refuse the offer and excused herself from the evening meal. The day had been draining, and she could not face the man she was to marry or the need to maintain inane polite conversation.

She did not sleep; she just lay on her bed thinking of what her future was going to be. She was disturbed by the knock she had agreed upon with Joseph and hurried to the door. "Hello?" she asked.

"Eleanor?" came the worried voice of Joseph.

Eleanor opened the door to reveal the concerned face of the man she loved. He entered the room and locked the door behind him. "I've heard the news," Joseph said, enveloping her in his arms.

For the first time that day Eleanor relaxed. She sagged against him. "You came," she murmured into his shoulder. She had not been sure he would return.

"Tell me about it," Joseph said, kissing the top of her head.

Eleanor lifted her head and looked at Joseph. "No, I want to forget. It will achieve nothing but make us both miserable. I want the next seven nights to be the happiest of my life. They have to be, Joe."

"They will be," Joseph said, kissing her passionately. "I love you, and I want you to be mine forever."

"I will for all intents and purposes; I may not carry your name, but I will carry you in here," Eleanor said touching her chest.

"I love you, Eleanor," Joseph said, picking her up and carrying her to the bed. He spent the next few hours showing her just how much.

*

The following morning Eleanor felt slightly different when Joseph left her room. There was a moment's panic when she realised there were now only six days left before she married, but she pushed it to one side. She would not spoil her time with Joseph.

A knock at her door startled her, and she approached the door cautiously. "Hello?" she said through the door.

"Eleanor, it's me," came Annabelle's clear voice.

Eleanor breathed a sigh of relief and opened the door, allowing her sister access. Annabelle looked concerned, but moved to a chaise lounge; she did not sit on it but stood behind it, gripping the back for support.

"I thought I would come and make sure you are well," Annabelle started, looking uncomfortable.

"I'm very well, thank you," Eleanor replied. She was, thanks to another night spent with the man she loved.

"Eleanor, you are taking a huge risk," Annabelle said with a sigh; she held up one of her hands to stop Eleanor interrupting. "I would have been here a minute or two earlier, only I rounded the corner to see Mr Heaton leaving your room."

"Oh," Eleanor replied.

"Yes, 'oh'," Annabelle said. "What if it had been father? You are playing a dangerous game the week before your wedding."

"I'm not," Eleanor said defiantly. "Father told Joseph that even if he compromised me the marriage to Mr Wadeson would go ahead, so I decided to take matters into my own hands and choose the man I love before I am forced into a marriage with a man who has yet to speak to me."

"Perhaps now would be a good time?" came a voice from the doorway.

Both women were startled at the voice, but their feelings turned to horror when they saw Mr Wadeson standing at the door. He smiled, but the expression held nothing but malevolence. "Yes, I too have seen your lover leaving your chamber these past two days."

Eleanor looked horrified, but spoke defiantly. "Luckily for me the door was locked when you tried it."

"Eleanor!" Annabelle hissed. She was too fully aware of what Mr Wadeson was capable of. She was terrified he would be even more vindictive when he finally married Eleanor.

Mr Wadeson laughed. "I'm glad to see more than one of the Johnson girls has spirit. I enjoyed crushing hers," he indicated Annabelle. "And now it seems I will have as much fun with you. Now should I wait until our marriage or should I make you return to your bed and take you where you can still smell your lover's scent? Wouldn't that be interesting the next time he came to visit? All you would think about would be me when he approached you. Yes, I think I like that idea."

He took a step forward, but Annabelle grabbed Eleanor and stood in front of her sister. "You are a sick person to take pleasure in inflicting pain on others. I won't let you hurt her!" Annabelle said.

"Remember our time together Annabelle?" Mr Wadeson said, smiling at the fact that Annabelle was defying him. "Remember just how it felt when I hit you? I wasn't angry then and yet you cried in pain, didn't you, my dear? If you don't move aside, I will get very angry, and I will hurt you, and then I will really hurt your sister."

Eleanor felt Annabelle shaking. She could not put her through any more horror than she already had been through. She stepped to the side of her sister. "You can do want you want with me, but let Annabelle go. You're not going to touch her ever again."

There was a movement at the door that went unnoticed by Mr Wadeson as he had his back to the door. Neither woman made a sound to indicate someone was entering the room.

"But what if I want to touch her again? I have happy memories of that time; it was a pity we didn't have more nights before you ran off to your sister. Perhaps Eleanor could watch and learn?"

"You will not lay a finger on her, or I will scream until someone comes running. I won't let you touch her," Eleanor said, trying to keep him talking.

"And how are you going to prevent it?" Mr Wadeson asked.

"She isn't, but I am," came the menacing growl of Lord Stannage.

Chapter 16

Frederick, Lord Stannage, had felt anger before in his life. He had been born with one green eye and one blue, which had given many of his peers a perfect reason to bully and torment a boy who was different. He had hated the bullies and had endured their taunts and beatings until he had decided it was time to fight back.

He had learned how to box, but he had also sought out a fighting coach not used by members of the ton. He was wise enough to realise going to the boxing masters his peers also were taught by gave him no real advantage. He found a man who improved on his technique, making sure when he was forced into a fight, he would come out victorious.

The ability to win, resulted in two things: the first was the physical bullying stopped. For young men, there was not much fun in losing a fight every time they went too far, and Frederick retaliated. The second benefit was that he was a calmer person. The physical exertion it took to take part in the type of fighting he practised drained him of any anger or angst he had struggled with in the past. So, Frederick appeared to be one of the most easy-going members of society, although that society was still cruel towards his eyes.

He had known anger more intense than he had ever experienced before when his wife had finally confided in him about what had happened in her past. They had had a difficult start to their marriage; he had presumed her rejection was because of her dislike of him until eventually she had told him the truth.

He had felt sickened to his stomach when she had tearfully told him about what had happened. Annabelle had presumed he would reject her once she had told her sordid secret, but he was a better man than that. He had wanted to kill the man who had inflicted such suffering on his wife but, towards her, he felt nothing but compassion and sympathy.

Little by little they had worked together, and she had overcome her dread of physical contact until she was as loving and responsive as he had hoped. Her nightmares had stopped, and she had regained some of the mischievous personality he had heard, before she had been attacked, was a very large part of her.

He had almost needed restraining when Mr Wadeson had been introduced into their midst his anger had been so strong, but Annabelle had begged him not to react.

"He will enjoy knowing you know," she said as Frederick raged.

"So, what am I to do? Say nothing, and he gets away with hurting and forcing himself on you?" Frederick had raged.

"If you say anything, it will no longer be a secret, and everyone will despise me," Annabelle had cried.

Frederick stopped his pacing and crouched before his wife. "No one would despise you," he said gently. "Annabelle, what he did was wrong; he cannot be allowed to get away with it."

"I don't want the shame," Annabelle had pleaded.

Frederick sat near his wife and wrapped her in his arms. She was so vulnerable because of one evil individual, and he could not get any sort of justice for her. He could never refuse such a heartfelt request. He held her until she calmed and then he lifted her arms off his shoulders to enable him to look into her eyes.

"Annabelle, there is one thing I feel you must do, or you will never forgive yourself," he had said gently.

"What is it?" she had asked wiping the tears away.

"You must tell your sisters what happened." He had leaned over and kissed her to reassure her; she gasped in horror at his words. "They are not safe with him in the house because they don't realise what he is capable of. Eleanor is especially at risk, because he thinks he is to marry her; I can't imagine he is the type of man to wait for his wedding night," Frederick continued gently.

"What will they think of me?" Annabelle asked, acknowledging she must do as Frederick suggested.

"They will be sorry you had to endure such an ordeal, but they will not think less of you. If you are being honest with yourself, you know that to be the case."

So, Annabelle had told her sisters, and Eleanor had been able to protect herself; but she had also made the decision to lie with Joseph as a consequence, something that Mr Wadeson was using to his advantage.

Frederick had followed his wife, whether it was a sixth sense or just his dislike of being separated from her, he did not know. He arrived at the corner of the hallway in time to see Mr Wadeson enter the room. His stomach turned, and he had to hold onto a table to prevent himself from charging into the room immediately after the man, but he had enough sense to wait.

This was the perfect opportunity for Frederick to give back some of the treatment Mr Wadeson seemed keen to give out as long as it was to someone who could not fight back.

Mr Wadeson turned at the sound of Frederick's voice, and he smiled a smug smile. "Well, well, well, if it isn't the freak come to protect his lovely wife."

Frederick did not respond; he had learned to watch and wait when dealing with bullies. To respond in the first instance very often showed your hand to the opponent you were facing.

"Not such a man after all, eh?" Mr Wadeson demanded with a sneer. "You picked the wrong husband," he said turning to Annabelle. "At least with me you already know I have some balls."

Frederick lunged at Mr Wadeson, knocking him to the floor. While Wadeson might be rotund, he was no pushover and was soon on his feet, throwing punches that were connecting with Frederick's body and face. The men battled moving backwards and forwards across the bedchamber as if it were a boxing ring.

Annabelle and Eleanor clung to each other, flinching every time a punch was landed. Neither were foolish enough to try and stop the fight; they knew Frederick needed to win for far more than just the slur on his masculinity.

Minutes passed without any let up from either side. Mr Wadeson had a severe cut over his eye, but Frederick's cheek was bleeding badly. Annabelle roused herself; it had to stop.

"Eleanor, go and fetch Peter!" she said urgently.

"I'm not leaving you here!" Eleanor did not wish to seem disloyal, but if Mr Wadeson gained the advantage over Frederick, goodness knows what he would inflict on Annabelle.

"I am not leaving Frederick," Annabelle said firmly. "You would never leave Mr Heaton; don't expect me to leave Freddy, but we need Peter!"

Eleanor nodded and carefully edged around the room until she reached the door. Once through it she ran to Rosalind's bedchamber. It was still relatively early, and she knew Peter shared Rosalind's room rather than using his own. She banged on the door, the need for urgency removing any decorum she might normally have shown. She hesitated from walking straight in; she did not wish to cause embarrassment for any of them, but she desperately needed a response from them.

She heard a voice and opened the door. Peter was walking across the room, tucking his shirt into his breeches; he paused when he saw the expression on Eleanor's face. "What is it?" he asked, grabbing a waistcoat and throwing it on.

"Frederick and Mr Wadeson are having an almighty battle in my room. Mr Wadeson was threatening all sorts of violence and worse to myself and Annabelle; Frederick overheard it," Eleanor babbled.

"Why are they in your room?" Peter asked, pulling his boots on.

Eleanor blushed, but spoke quickly, there was no time to lose. "Mr Wadeson has been trying to get access to my chamber, although I didn't realise he was also watching it. Annabelle had come to see if I was well. Both of them saw Joseph leaving my chamber."

Peter's eyes flickered to Eleanor's, and her blush deepened, but she did not see condemnation in his expression. He stood and moved to leave the room. Eleanor followed him, but Peter put his hand on her arm. "Stay here. I need to know where you are. There is going to be fall-out because of what you told me; I can't imagine a man like Wadeson keeping quiet about what you have been doing."

"Oh," Eleanor said, realising life was going to become even more uncomfortable, but then she remembered Annabelle. "He may hurt Annabelle," she said, once more moving to leave the room.

"I know, Eleanor," Peter said softly. Eleanor looked at him. "He won't get to her, not while there is breath in Frederick's or my body," he said gently.

Eleanor nodded and stepped back, allowing Peter to leave the room. She turned to her sister who had been quiet through the exchange and saw her smile slightly at her.

"I think you'd better tell me what's been going on," Rosalind said, patting the side of the bed that was now empty. "I would imagine we had best get a plan together before father comes rampaging through the house looking for you."

Eleanor went gratefully to her sister and told her everything, including how she felt and what was troubling her. She was not used to keeping secrets from Rosalind, and it felt a relief to be able to speak about it.

*

Peter returned to Rosalind's bedchamber some thirty minutes later. His clothing was bloody, but there did not appear to be any marks on his face. Rosalind and Eleanor had remained on the bed talking things over, and both let out exclamations of worry at Peter's attire.

"Don't worry yourself, this is Mr Wadeson's blood," Peter said, taking a seat in relief.

"And that is supposed to reassure us?" Rosalind said drily.

Peter smiled. "I suppose not. Mr Wadeson came off the worse from the encounter, and I can't say I'm sorry for it. He may think twice when hurting someone related to Frederick in the future."

"How is Frederick?" Eleanor asked, worriedly.

"He'll be sporting some interesting colours once the bruising develops, but he hasn't suffered any permanent injuries," Peter reassured them both.

"What about Annabelle? She must be beside herself after witnessing a fight," Rosalind said with a shudder.

"She's purely concerned with how Frederick is," Peter said. "To be honest, it was good to witness her concern. I know they have seemed happy enough while they have been here but, with the rocky start to their marriage, I did wonder. I'm under no doubt now; she is clearly besotted with him, and I'm glad. Frederick deserves to be happy."

"I'm relieved they are both well," Rosalind said.

"Yes, although Annabelle said we probably won't see them for the rest of the day. She is insisting Frederick have complete bed rest, at least for today. He tried to insist he was well, but she was not listening," Peter said in amusement.

"Mr Wadeson?" Eleanor asked tentatively. She was not really interested in his welfare, but what happened to him unfortunately had an impact on the others in the family, especially her.

"I carried him to his room and sent for water and cloths. I refuse to put members of staff at risk of him, so I told him he must treat himself or arrange his own nurse. I did suggest he seek help from your father," Peter said with a small smile. "But he didn't seem too enamoured with that suggestion for some reason."

"Father will find out about this; there is no doubt," Rosalind said.

"He will, but I have a few things to say to your father myself," Peter said grimly.

Rosalind and Eleanor decided wisely it was probably best to not to question what Peter intended to say.

*

Peter did not wish to visit Mr Wadeson at all, but propriety led him to his guest's room later that afternoon. The man was propped up in bed, barely moving. His face was a mass of cuts and bruises, and his eyes were beginning to close because of the swelling.

Peter did not open the conversation with concern about his welfare; he was not a man to lie. "You have behaved in the worse possible way while staying as a guest in my house. I do not take kindly to such disrespect to myself or my family," he said sternly.

Before Mr Wadeson could reply the door opened, and Mr Johnson entered the room. "Good god man, what on earth foolery is this?" Mr Johnson said at Mr Wadeson's appearance.

"Your protégé decided he was going to inflict harm on two of your daughters; thankfully Frederick arrived before any harm was done and dealt his own punishment as you can see," Peter said grimly.

"What has got into you? Could you not wait a week before the marriage?" Mr Johnson asked Mr Wadeson.

"They were making a fool out of me," Mr Wadeson muttered, not able to speak properly.

"I think the time for planning a marriage has passed," Peter said.

"Why?" Mr Johnson asked sharply.

Peter looked at the man astounded. "Surely you are not considering allowing the marriage to continue?" he asked incredulously.

"One mistake does not warrant the marriage being cancelled. It is a good match for Eleanor," Mr Johnson insisted.

Peter looked dumbfounded. Rosalind had told him what Annabelle had been forced to endure, and he thought it appropriate Mr Johnson be told of the reality of Mr Wadeson's character. "He forced himself on Annabelle when he thought they were to be married. He likes to inflict pain on those he lies with. Now he has spent the last few days trying to gain access to Eleanor's bedchamber. Do you honestly wish your daughter to be connected to such a man?"

Mr Johnson paused. It was clear he had not known what had occurred between Mr Wadeson and his daughters. His colour faded a little, but he looked Peter in the eye. "Eleanor will marry Wadeson," he said quietly.

"Thank God, most of your daughter's no longer need your protection; at least they are safe. God help Eleanor; you are condemning her to a life that doesn't bare thinking about! I hope your decision keeps you awake at night."

"You weren't being so disrespectful when you wanted my money," Mr Johnson said defiantly.

"It is not a case of being disrespectful; I am trying to protect your daughter, a pity you can't," Peter responded. "I wish you and your puppet to leave tomorrow. I will not be a part of this, although I insist that Eleanor stays with us until the wedding."

"What, so there can be more liaisons with the Duke sniffing around her?" Mr Wadeson growled.

"I shall be asking him to leave today," Peter said sharply. "I do not wish for anyone in my household to behave inappropriately no matter who they are."

Peter left the room with no respect remaining for either gentlemen. He went to speak to Joseph; he was going to ask him to leave, but not for the reason he had stated. A plan was forming in his mind, and he needed Joseph to co-operate with him for it to work.

Mr Johnson turned to Mr Wadeson when the door closed behind Peter. "Are you a complete fool?" he asked.

Mr Wadeson's eyes sparkled with menace. "Remember who you are talking too. I may have to put up with the likes of his sanctimonious words, but I don't with you."

For once Mr Johnson snapped at the man before him. "You forced yourself on one of my daughters, and you ask me to watch what I am saying?" he asked in disbelief.

"Is it my fault you let her go off and marry someone else? As far as I knew she was to be my wife," Mr Wadeson replied, showing no remorse.

"I don't think this is a good idea anymore," Mr Johnson started, before the glare from Mr Wadeson stopped him from continuing.

It hurt every time Mr Wadeson spoke, but he was determined to put Mr Johnson back under his control. "It doesn't matter whether you think it is a good idea or not; the deal for my silence was one of your daughters. The wedding will go ahead, unless you wish the whole of your family to find out what you have been doing."

Mr Johnson paled again, "You can't keep threatening me with that for the rest of my life!"

"I can, but once I've married and had your business handed over to me officially, I think it is time you retired to somewhere warm," Mr Wadeson said.

"I'm not going to retire!" Mr Johnson almost shouted. All that was precious to him was related to work, and the panic he felt at it being taken away from him almost took his breath away.

"Oh, yes, you are; it's time for a change, I think. I've had you moaning around me for too long now; I'm sick of the delays and sick of you. Mrs Johnson will enjoy a trip to the West Indies, I think; it will do you both the world of good."

"I wish I'd never set eyes on you!" Mr Johnson spat, knowing he could not argue against anything his nemesis demanded.

"You should have stuck to an honest income and not been so greedy, and you wouldn't have," Mr Wadeson said unsympathetically.

"One day Wadeson, you'll regret meeting me," Mr Johnson threatened.

Mr Wadeson smirked as much as his injuries would let him. "If you had any way of getting rid of me, you would have done it by now. No, things are still going to end as I want; I marry your daughter and get handed your business. How much she gets beaten will depend on how good you are to me; if you moan at me all day, I will arrive home very angry."

Mr Johnson looked sickened and left the bedchamber. He was at a loss as to how his circumstances could change in such a short period of time. Wadeson was right; there was nothing he could do but hand over his daughter and business and watch both be destroyed. He hoped Eleanor could forgive him if she ever found out the truth, but he was not sure if he would ever be able to forgive himself.

Chapter 17

Peter left Joseph's bedchamber. It had not been an easy conversation as, once he explained what Mr Wadeson had done, Joseph had to be physically restrained from going and finishing the job Frederick had started.

"If you do anything to him, it will ruin Eleanor," Peter said, not releasing Joseph until he relaxed from the tension currently straining against his arms.

"It won't matter; I will marry her," Joseph snarled.

"For some unknown reason Mr Johnson won't agree to it," Peter said, the fact still not making any sense to him. "You have to accept she isn't yours."

Joseph slumped, the fight going out of him. "I don't know how I'm going to carry on if her marriage goes ahead."

Peter had some sympathy with Joseph; it was obvious he adored Eleanor. "We'll deal with that when we have to, but for now I need you to leave."

Joseph had frowned at him. "Don't do this."

"I have to; you have behaved inappropriately in my house: I cannot allow you to stay," Peter had said firmly.

Joseph looked at him and wondered if he had changed over the years; he had never seemed so unyielding. "She said we were to be together until her marriage took place. How can I leave behind the promise of some happiness, however temporary?"

"You must, but I think you will approve of where I want you to stay," Peter said and went on to explain his plan to Joseph.

*

Bryant was at his post in the hallway when Mrs Adams called to pay her morning visit. "Good morning, madam," Bryant said with a slight bow.

"Morning Bryant. Is the Duchess still above stairs, enjoying the reprieve from receiving the local fools?" Mrs Adams would never approve of most of the people in her neighbourhood.

Bryant never flickered in response, but he was in complete agreement with Mrs Adams's opinion of most of the locality. "His Grace would like a word with you before you join Her Grace; if you would be so kind as to follow me?"

"Oh, really? What's amiss now?" Mrs Adams muttered half to herself as she was led to Peter's study.

Peter looked up from his desk and smiled as Mrs Adams entered. "Good morning!" he said, standing and going to greet her. "I'm glad you've arrived; we have a lot to talk about."

"What have you done wrong this time?" Mrs Adams said, taking a seat.

Peter smiled. "It will always warm my heart the way you always presume the worst from me," he said with amusement. He was fully aware of Mrs Adams's high regard for him.

"Harrumph," came the response, but there was a twinkle in her eyes.

"So, to business," Peter said, returning to his seat. "I'm sorry to say that tomorrow you are going to injure your back."

Mrs Adams looked suspiciously at Peter. "I beg your pardon?" she asked. "There is nothing wrong with my back. What tomfoolery is this?"

"A back injury is very serious, I shall have you know, in a lady of your advanced years," Peter said and started to explain exactly what was on his mind.

*

Eleanor was summoned to say goodbye to her father. She had been in her room heartbroken over Joseph leaving before she had the opportunity to say goodbye to him. Peter had been firm with her; she was not to see him before he left, and it was impossible for Joseph to stay after what had happened.

The thought of not seeing him again devastated her, and she had not been able to keep the tears from streaming down her face as she argued with Peter. Eventually she had accepted defeat and spent the next hour in her bedchamber, crying into her pillow.

Peter had sent a summons to her to join him downstairs. She reluctantly complied, but he had wrapped her in an embrace, kissing the top of her head. "Forgive me, Eleanor," he said gently. "Your father and Mr Wadeson are leaving, and it is important you say goodbye to them."

"No!" Eleanor wailed, the tears starting again. "Please, Peter! I don't wish to see either of them."

Peter took hold of Eleanor's face between his hands and forced her to look at him. "Trust me, Eleanor; I would not be doing this unless it was important. I'm going to be inviting your father for supper tonight; I need you to be there."

"I don't wish to speak to him," Eleanor said defiantly.

"I'm not asking you to, just be there, and you will see him tomorrow as well," Peter said.

"Why?" Eleanor asked, feeling Peter was showing a cruel streak she had not seen previously.

"Trust me, Eleanor," was all Peter said in response.

They went into the hallway to see the flurry of activity the leaving of guests created. Mr Johnson had seen the Duke of Adlington leave and was not surprised his youngest daughter looked devastated. He felt some remorse, but Mr Wadeson was watching him from the seat he had been led to, so Mr Johnson decided against trying to comfort his daughter. It would only increase her suffering at Mr Wadeson's hands.

"Mr Johnson, please join us for supper tonight," Peter said amenably. "Mr Wadeson, the invitation does not extend to you."

Eleanor was surprised Peter did not drop down dead, the venom in the look that Mr Wadeson sent him was so strong. Mr Johnson nodded his head and hurried the footmen along. The faster they left the building, the less Mr Wadeson could get upset.

"The Crown do a reasonable meal," Peter continued referring to the hostelry that was located a mile away. "The beds are clean and no undesirables frequent there."

"Until now," Eleanor muttered and received a smile of appreciation from Peter.

"We shall see you at six, Mr Johnson," he said and turned away, directing Eleanor into the drawing room. They left the gentlemen to remove themselves from the building without further delay.

*

Mr Johnson arrived promptly. He had been sent to check on Eleanor by Mr Wadeson and, in some respects, had wanted to see her himself. He was surprised when entering the dining room, he saw Rosalind seated at the head of the table.

"Isn't it a little early for you to be leaving your chamber after your confinement?" he asked his eldest daughter.

"With the events of the past day, I thought it best to come and offer my support to my sisters," Rosalind said coolly.

Grace and Harry had not joined the family, so a subdued Frederick and Annabelle joined Eleanor, Rosalind, Peter and Mr Johnson. There was little talking, and less frivolity; none of the three sisters could forgive their father for lack of support, but they could not openly voice their opinion.

Frederick, Peter and Mr Johnson shared a glass of port when the ladies withdrew. Conversation was stilted, but Mr Johnson decided he needed to get something off his chest.

"What is the meaning of the Duke of Adlington staying at the Crown?" Mr Johnson asked Peter.

"Is he?" Peter responded. "He's a fool for staying close; he won't get access to this house."

"I hope there is no funny business going on," Mr Johnson said as surly as a spoiled child.

"Have you seen the state of your daughter?" Peter said with derision. "I don't think she has stopped crying since I demanded that Joseph leave the building and not return. She looks to me as if she has accepted her fate, the poor thing."

"Yes, well, I have made my decision," Mr Johnson said uncomfortably.

"We are well aware of that," Peter said grimly.

As Mr Johnson was leaving, Peter invited him to breakfast with them and then he would take him fishing. Mr Johnson accepted on two points, it would take him away from Mr Wadeson and he thought that if his secret did emerge, it may be wise to have the friendship of some of his relations.

Eleanor hardly slept. She hoped that Joseph would find a way to gain access to the house and reach her, but no knock came on the door. She eventually fell into a fitful sleep, wondering if the pain would ever go away.

When morning came, she looked into the looking glass with a groan. The dark rings under her eyes were visible to even her tear-filled eyes. She sighed, dressing in a plain cotton gown. There was little point in making an effort with her dress or hair. She had never felt beautiful until she had met Joseph. For those precious moments she had felt like the most beautiful person in the world, but more than that, she felt treasured and loved. With it now being ripped away, all that was left was desolation.

She joined the others at breakfast. Grace had joined the family and embraced her sister when she entered the dining room. Mr Johnson was already seated, not commenting, but watching the exchange.

"Eleanor, you will rally," Grace whispered.

"I'm not sure I want to," Eleanor whispered back.

Peter joined the group and they sat eating in almost silence. The bread tasted like powder to Eleanor, every piece seeming to stick in her throat. Mr Johnson turned to speak to Peter. "A gentleman left the Crown this morning. He sent his best wishes to you, although he is not intending visiting again anytime soon. I was glad to see him leave."

Eleanor looked alert, but Peter indicated that she should not say anything. "I can't imagine what would bring him to the area anytime in the future. Shall we collect our fishing tackle, Mr Johnson?"

It was many hours before the gentlemen returned. Rosalind was poised, ready to serve tea and cakes to her father, inviting Eleanor to join them. Peter was given a missive by Bryant and he read in silence for a moment.

Peter turned to Rosalind. "Have you heard from Mrs Adams today?"

"No, I was surprised that she did not join us at the end of morning visits, she usually does. I just presumed that she was preparing for the new Mr and Mrs Adams returning from their wedding trip," Rosalind replied.

"It seems not," Peter said, indicating the letter in his hand. "She has had a fall and hurt her back."

"Oh no!" Rosalind cried. "We must go to her!"

"Yes, I think that is a good idea, but she asks for specific help," Peter said.

"What is it? The poor woman must be in agony to be asking for help. I have never met a more proud being," Rosalind said compassionately.

"She asks if Eleanor or Annabelle could stay with her for a few days until Frances and Stuart return," Peter explained.

"I'll stay," Rosalind said.

"I think you are forgetting that little bundle of ours," Peter said with a smile. "Luckily Mrs Adams hasn't, which is why she has asked for Annabelle or Eleanor."

"I'll go," Eleanor said quietly.

"You'll do no such thing!" Mr Johnson said hastily. "You are to be married in four days, Mrs Adams must have forgotten."

"She's the only one that has," Eleanor said bitterly.

Peter thought it wise to intervene when he saw Mr Johnson's thunderous expression. "Mrs Adams expects her son and daughter-in-law in two days, hence the specific request. There is nothing to do for preparation of the wedding that we can't do, Eleanor does not need to be here for the preparations to continue. It will keep Eleanor occupied, save her dwelling on the future," Peter reasoned.

"I shall accompany you," Rosalind said. "I won't be happy until I have seen her. I expect she has refused to send for the doctor."

"I shall arrange the carriage," Peter said. "Shall we say half an hour?"

Rosalind and Eleanor left the room to change into their outerwear before meeting in the hallway. "Ready?" Rosalind asked and left the house at Eleanor's nod.

Both women climbed into the carriage and it set off at a smart pace. Eleanor had packed a small trunk and Rosalind had packed some items that she insisted that Mrs Adams would need. Eleanor thought that it was a little excessive, but she knew that her sister was a carer, so did not question her.

They travelled in silence. Eleanor felt completely drained and did not really think she had the energy to look after an invalid for the next two days, but at least she would be away from her father. She was not sure that she would ever be able to forgive him for what he was forcing her to do.

Rosalind watched Eleanor, her heart aching for the pain she had been forced to endure over the last day. She was not sure if she would survive a separation from Peter at this point in their lives, but Eleanor faced a future that was very dark, making what she had lost seem even more devastating.

The carriage drew to a stop outside the Adams household. Rosalind stepped down and waited until her sister stepped from the carriage. She linked Eleanor's arm as they walked into the house. When Rosalind had handed her bonnet and gloves to the footman, she took Eleanor's hand, who looked at her in surprise.

"I love you Eleanor and I want you to be happy," Rosalind said, not waiting for a response and led the way into the morning room.

Eleanor followed with a frown on her face. Mrs Adams was lying on her sofa, looking comfortable. She noticed Eleanor's frown and smiled.

"So the thought of two days with me and your expression resembles that of a thunder cloud," Mrs Adams said cheerfully.

"Not at all," Eleanor said quickly. "I am happy to be here and do anything that will help you."

"I would love to have you here," Mrs Adams said fondly. "I have thoroughly enjoyed all my dealings with you girls, you've been a bright addition to my life," she continued expressing what she felt but would rarely say.

"Did you hit your head when you fell?" Rosalind asked with a smile.

Mrs Adams laughed and stood up. Eleanor looked in question, "Won't you damage your back by moving?" she asked, but Mrs Adams did not appear to have any more trouble than normal when she moved.

"I was quite surprised when Peter said that I was going to have a fall and hurt my back," Mrs Adams said with a chuckle. "When he explained further, I was quite impressed, I'd never expected him to be quite so devious."

"Rosalind?" Eleanor said in doubt and a sliver of hope.

"Come in Mr Heaton!" Mrs Adams shouted through the closed door.

Joseph walked through the door, looking as well as could be expected after a tense two days. He took one look at Eleanor and crossed the room to her, pulling her into his arms. "I've missed you Eleanor."

Chapter 18

Eleanor should have been ladylike and swooned when the love of her life returned to her. She should have put her hand to her forehead and said some profound words that they would both treasure for the rest of their lives. She did none of that, she wrapped her arms around his neck and burst into tears.

Joseph held her close, gently stroking her back until she calmed down. Eventually she was able to control herself enough to wipe her face and look at him without crying again. "I must look a sight," she hiccupped.

"You do," Mrs Adams said.

Joseph smiled at Eleanor. "You look like my beautiful girl and I am never letting you out of my sight again. This last day has been pure torture. I was only able to bear it because I knew that fiend was incapable of doing you any harm."

"I marry him in a few days," Eleanor said, her eyes filling with tears once more.

"Oh no you don't," Rosalind interrupted. Eleanor looked at her sister, the hope that sprung into her eyes, was proof to Rosalind that they were all doing the right thing. "You are to marry Mr Heaton. I am not to be the only Duchess in the family!" she smiled.

"A dash to the border?" Eleanor asked. "Father is determined for the marriage to take place, he will follow us."

"Yes, but my husband is a genius," Rosalind said with a grin. "Everyone will expect you to make a dash for the border, so Peter suggested to Mr Heaton that he organise a special licence."

"Peter thought of everything," Joseph said. "I was too intent on killing Mr Wadeson to think straight, but thankfully Peter kept calm."

"He's his mother's son," Mrs Adams chipped in with pride at her deceased best friend's boy.

"He told me to leave the house and organise a special licence. Then I had to book rooms at the Crown and make sure that I saw Mr Johnson. Your father had to see me leave this morning, so that you would be seen by him at a far later time. It was all contrived to make the suspicion of us eloping together more remote," Joseph explained.

"He then hid out with me, while I had to pretend that I'd fallen and needed you for two days. That way tonight your absence would not be missed," Mrs Adams chipped in, not wanting to be left out.

"So, later today my darling Eleanor, we are to be married and then commence our journey to my home, south of here. No one will presume that we have travelled south," Joseph said, kissing Eleanor's hand.

"Annabelle and Grace will miss your wedding, but I hope the presence of myself and Mrs Adams will go some way to compensate for their absence," Rosalind said.

"But my things…." Eleanor started.

"Are all in the carriage," Rosalind interrupted. "I noticed you looking at the luggage and prayed that you did not mention anything. I needed the amount of luggage that I was bringing not to be noticed. Bryant is a real gem when deviousness is required," Rosalind said, pleased at the abilities of the long-term butler.

"I'm not sure he would appreciate that label," Mrs Adams said. "Right, we have all wasted enough time. Are you ready to go to your wedding, my dear?" she asked Eleanor.

"Oh yes!" Eleanor responded, squeezing Joseph's hand.

*

Rosalind and Mrs Adams rode in the Duke's carriage, allowing Eleanor and Joseph some time alone before they reached the ceremony. It would be an hour's travel before they reached the chapel that Joseph had made arrangements with.

As soon as the carriage had started, Joseph pulled Eleanor onto his knee. Eleanor laughed, it felt strange to her ears, she had not expected to feel like laughing for a long time, when she had awoken a few hours previously.

"I think I would have committed murder if your marriage to that man had gone ahead," Joseph said, his frown prominent and his eyes dark with menace. "When Peter said what had happened after I had left your chamber, I had never felt so angry in my life."

Eleanor kissed him gently. "It doesn't matter now, he won't affect us any longer. I thought I would never see you again."

"It doesn't matter now, but there is one important thing we haven't discussed," Joseph said with a smile.

"What's that?"

"I feel as if I am kidnapping you," he said with a grin. "We are travelling to the church where we will marry, and I haven't found out yet if you will marry me."

Eleanor smiled. "How long have we until we arrive?"

"Less than an hour."

"That should give you enough time to persuade me," Eleanor responded, wrapping her arms around Joseph's neck. "I have ached since I saw you last. I never want to be separated from you again."

There was no further talk in the carriage; there was only time for their love to be expressed in actions rather than words.

*

Rosalind returned to Sudworth Hall during the early evening. She was exhausted and immediately returned to her bedchamber. The first journey after confinement had been a long one, and her body was complaining about the exertion. She would not have had it any other way. She had been able to see all three of her sisters married to the men they loved. It went some way to compensate for the fact they had not been present at her wedding.

She was joined by Grace and Annabelle, who had been told by Peter what had happened. They were surprised, but pleased Eleanor had finally been able to marry Joseph.

"When will Father find out?" Annabelle asked.

"Peter is going to speak to him tomorrow," Rosalind replied. "I'm hoping he just accepts it, but he has seemed unnaturally insistent that Eleanor marry Mr Wadeson."

"I don't know why; father is no fool: surely he sees what we all do?" Annabelle mused.

"He appears to like him," Grace said. "But mother didn't. They had arguments about him, more so after you married, Annabelle."

"Something isn't right, but I have no idea what," Rosalind mused.

*

Peter decided to speak to Mr Johnson after they shared lunch the following day. Joseph and Eleanor would have been married for a day and well on their way to Joseph's estate. He asked Frederick to join him for the meeting, hoping together they could reassure Mr Johnson the outcome was the best for all parties.

Mr Johnson had other ideas though and raised the subject during lunch, when Annabelle and Grace were with the group. "When is Eleanor expected to return? Mr Wadeson insists on seeing her today; he has details he wishes to discuss with her."

Rosalind looked slightly alarmed, but Peter remained unfazed. "She is helping our friend, as she was yesterday," Peter replied.

"If you could give me the direction, I need to take her to Wadeson; I can return her afterwards," Mr Johnson insisted.

Peter indicated the staff should leave and waited until the door had closed behind them before speaking once more. His tone was calm enough, but there was a no-nonsense edge to it. "Eleanor will not be visiting Mr Wadeson now or any time in the future."

"I beg your pardon?" Mr Johnson spluttered. "I shall remind you she may be staying as your guest, but she is very much my daughter."

"Whom you are willing to give up as a living sacrifice to a man you must know is totally unsuitable for any female, let alone your own daughter," Peter said sternly.

Mr Johnson's face was very red, anger bubbling from every pore. Rosalind thought she could detect something else in her father's demeanour, and it was something she was surprised to see: it was fear.

"Father, surely after everything that has happened, you should be considering ending your association with Mr Wadeson?" Rosalind asked quietly.

"Rosalind, you have no idea how business works; please do not interfere," Mr Johnson snapped. He turned back to Peter. "I demand you give me the address where Eleanor is staying."

"I don't know where she is staying," Peter said with a shrug. It was time to be honest. "She was handed over to the care of the Duke of Adlington yesterday with all our blessings."

Mr Johnson jumped up from the chair so quickly the chair was sent clattering back, landing upside down on the wooden floor. "You've done what?!" he shouted. "Good God, man! You've ruined me!"

Mr Johnson stormed around the dining room, muttering to himself and cursing. The three Johnson women were mortified at his behaviour, but Rosalind looked calm enough. "Father, sit; it is not so bad."

"It is worse than you could possibly know!" Mr Johnson spat. "I shall set off for the border. I need a horse, and I need it now!" he demanded of Peter.

Peter decided, although Mr Johnson had reacted in the way he had presumed he would, there was no point in allowing him to ride half way across the country in an effort to stop his daughter, who had never been on the route he would be travelling. Peter was not a cruel man and had some family loyalty to his wife's father. If it had been Mr Wadeson before him, he would have had no compunction in sending him out on a wild goose chase.

"Mr Johnson," Peter started. "Eleanor was married yesterday by special licence. They now are on their wedding trip, which I believe is to be a number of weeks. The Duke of Adlington did not specify particulars of where he intended to travel; looking at your response, a sensible precaution."

"Good God! It is worse than I thought. We will have to have the marriage annulled," Mr Johnson said, sinking into a spare chair.

"There are witnesses who will testify that will prevent the marriage being annulled. They had carnal knowledge of each other before they were wed; I'm afraid that hope is futile," Peter responded calmly, curious to know why there was such a poor reaction.

Mr Johnson looked at Peter, anguish in his expression. "I am ruined, and all my family will suffer as a consequence. You are so smug, yet you won't be so happy when all my daughters, my wife and myself are vilified in the newspapers, and I am thrown into Newgate, if not worse."

Peter was immediately on the alert. It had not made sense as to why Mr Johnson was so insistent about such an ill-matched wedding to take place, but now it seemed there were other reasons driving the man.

"Is it so bad?" he asked gently. It was not too long ago since he was facing the loss of his estate, so he had some sympathy with the man.

"It is worse," Mr Johnson said grimly.

"I suggest you tell us the truth, and then we'll know what we are facing," Peter said.

Mr Johnson sighed; they were going to find out: after he had told Wadeson Eleanor was married, there was no way the man would remain silent; they might as well have the extra time to prepare themselves. He started to speak, facing his daughters and dreading their condemnation.

"Wadeson was brought in to my business to boost trade. Things were slowing; the cost to bring in materials from abroad is increasing every week, so prices were going up and sales down. Other businesses were going out of trade, so something had to be done, or I would follow," Mr Johnson said, remembering the panic he had felt to see the businesses he had created start to flounder.

"What was his role?" Peter asked, keen to keep Mr Johnson focused.

Mr Johnson looked down, unable to see the disappointment in his daughters' eyes. "I was sending ships across the oceans, sometimes empty on one of the journeys, so a few times we arranged that the ships should be 'lost', enabling me to claim the insurance on a full ship even though it had been empty."

"What happened to the ships and those on board?" Peter asked.

"Nothing. I was not going to be responsible for murder, so we recruited sailors keen to leave the shores for a number of years. The ships were taken to a port and renamed and, after a time, the ships and their crew would return. I would sell the ships and make a profit in addition to receiving the insurance money," Mr Johnson explained. It had been so easy to achieve.

"How many times did you do it?" Frederick asked.

"Only twice," Mr Johnson admitted. "Any more and the insurers would have become suspicious. I'd thought that would be enough."

"It isn't anything to be proud of, but it is hardly a hanging offence," Peter said. Fraud would not be looked on kindly, but he was sure a prison sentence could be avoided.

"That isn't all," Mr Johnson admitted. "Losing two ships helped, but long-term there was still the downward trend, so Wadeson suggested we do something else."

"Go on," Peter said grimly. This was not going to be good if Wadeson had been the instigator of it.

"Slaves," Mr Johnson said quietly.

"Slaves?" Peter said, a lump forming in his stomach.

"Yes. It was profitable to fill the ship with a few hundred slaves, send them over to the plantations who still need slaves and then continue onto America for supplies," Mr Johnson said.

"Slaves?" Grace said, horrified.

Mr Johnson just nodded; he did not look at any of his daughters: he felt the tension increase in the room as he spoke.

"Transporting slaves is illegal," Annabelle said in confusion.

"It is, but it still goes on," Frederick explained to his wife. "It's still profitable for those willing to take the risk."

"I don't understand," Rosalind said frowning. "It is years since the law was changed. I remember all the fuss in the newspapers."

"It was probably over a decade ago now," Peter said. "But as Frederick said, it is still happening. How did you get past the West Africa Squadron?" he asked, referring to the squadron that patrolled the waters off West Africa to try and intercept ships breaking the law.

"Wadeson was the practical one. Bribes played a part; anyone can be bribed for the right price," Mr Johnson responded.

"Father, how could you get involved with something so immoral?" Annabelle exclaimed.

"You weren't saying that when you were spending the money earned from it!" Mr Johnson snapped, not one to take responsibility for his actions.

"You can have every penny you gave for Annabelle's dowry; we do not wish to have anything to do with dirty money," Frederick said sharply.

Peter was in a difficult position; he felt exactly the same as Frederick, only the money that had been supplied as part of Rosalind's dowry had saved the family estate. He was not sure how he was going to repay it, but he would have to find a way.

Mr Johnson looked at Frederick in disgust. "Do you think I would give my daughters dirty money? Their dowries have been in place since their births. I did take some out of Annabelle's, hence it was less than Rosalind's."

"You said that was because she was marrying a Lord and not a Duke," Peter reminded him.

"It was a convenient excuse," Mr Johnson admitted.

"And what about Grace's dowry?" Rosalind demanded. Her sister had not received anything from her father because she had married a gardener and not a titled gentleman.

"I don't want anything; I am perfectly happy with my lot," Grace said quickly.

"Wadeson has had most of it, but there is still some left I will send you. It is only fair you receive some money," Mr Johnson said. Grace was the most gentle of his daughters, and he knew without doubt she would struggle with what he had done.

"You said I didn't deserve any dowry for marrying Harry; what has changed?" Grace asked.

"I always wanted you all to marry titled gentlemen; it was a point of pride for me. I would have been so proud to say all my daughters were titled and then my grandchildren would have titles in their own right. I'd put money aside each time one of you was born; business was good then," Mr Johnson explained.

"Why did you change your mind and insist that one of us marry Mr Wadeson after Rosalind had married? It seemed such a complete about turn," Annabelle asked, trying to find out as much as possible during the one meaningful conversation any of them had ever had with their father.

"It was," Mr Johnson responded. "I'd never intended any of you marrying him. I didn't want him as part of the family. I was a fool to think he would just accept what I paid him. I hadn't realised he was using me as much as I was using him, only he was more cunning."

"That is hardly surprising," Rosalind said quietly.

"He has enough information to get me hanged," Mr Johnson responded.

"I do not condone what you have done," Peter said. "In fact the whole situation disgusts me, but if you are honest and pay the fines you would be given for the transportation of slaves, surely his hold over you would be at an end?"

"If it were only so simple," came the bleak reply. "You see, we didn't always escape the West Africa Squadron and rather than pay the fine, Wadeson and the crew threw the slaves overboard."

Chapter 19

The room was silent for many minutes. No one was quite sure how to respond to the information that had just been thrown into the room as surely as the slaves had been thrown overboard. Grace sat silently, tears running down her cheeks as she imagined the horror the defenceless slaves must have faced.

Finally Peter broke the silence. "Good God, what have you been a part of?"

"I had no idea he was going to do something like that!" Mr Johnson said, trying to defend the indefensible. "I was at home: he was the one who accompanied the ships; he was desperate to explore other ways of making money at the ports the ships visited. He made the decision; he ordered them thrown overboard, but of course that's not how he tells it."

"What happened to the slaves?" Rosalind asked, feeling as if her world had tilted upside down; she was seeing her father in such a different way than she had ever seen him before. There had never been much filial affection, but her feelings now meant any future relationship was probably completely irreparable.

Mr Johnson looked uncomfortable. "They wouldn't have been able to swim anyway," he replied, still defensive.

"That isn't an answer," Annabelle snapped at her father, hating him for what he had put them all through, and now it seemed hundreds of innocents as well.

"Wadeson said there was no time to unfasten the chains," Mr Johnson said.

"I can't listen to any more!" Grace cried, standing and covering her ears. "You murderer! How could you?"

"I didn't know until after it happened!" Mr Johnson said, looking pleadingly at Grace.

"You were in company with the devil, and yet you still went along with everything he said!" Annabelle said in disgust, standing to comfort Grace.

"Of course, I tried to argue against him! Do you think I have no morals? But he had gathered enough information that I could do nothing. When he returned from that trip he decided he wanted me to hand his business over to him, but he also wanted one of you," Mr Johnson explained his change about who should marry his daughters. "Rosalind was already married by then, so he had the choice of the three of you."

"He made that quickly enough," Annabelle said bitterly.

"I am sorry for what he did to you; I had no idea," Mr Johnson said, his eyes trying to express the remorse he felt.

"You wouldn't have stopped him even if you had, would you?" Annabelle said bitterly.

"Probably not," Mr Johnson said with some shame.

"I thought not. You are a spineless man!" Annabelle said with venom. "But do you know something? In some respects I'm thankful for what happened."

The others in the party looked in shock at Annabelle, knowing how much she had struggled and still did with what happened.

Annabelle smiled at the shock on their faces. "I would never have been struggling with my demons if it hadn't happened, and I would never have been in that study when Frederick was," she explained, glancing quickly at her husband. "I know the start of our marriage was not as either of us would have wished, but I am so proud to be your wife, and I can never regret marrying you." She had turned to face Frederick, but was still standing with Grace.

Frederick stood up and walked across to his wife, taking her into his arms. "I thank the day we met, and I will never cease being amazed you are my wife. I think it would be best if we left now. We've heard enough. Peter, if you need my assistance in anything, you have it; but I feel taking Grace and Annabelle out of here now would be the best thing I could do."

Peter nodded his agreement. Mr Johnson turned to his daughters. "I am truly sorry."

"It is not the right time to mention this; we were going to wait until after the hub-bub about Eleanor had died down, but we have news," Annabelle said looking at her father. "I am increasing and, whether this is a girl or boy, it will never know its grandparents."

"Annabelle, that is wonderful news, but surely now is not the time to make such a decision?" Rosalind asked gently.

"He was handing us over without fighting for us just because he was too weak to face the consequences. At any time he could have put a stop to it, and we would have been protected, but he chose himself over his children. I don't want anyone with that tendency anywhere near a child of ours," Annabelle said defiantly.

The threesome left the room without a look back. Mr Johnson looked crushed. "What she says is right. I did put myself above anyone else, and now it doesn't matter because, with Eleanor's elopement, all will be revealed anyway," he said.

"You're going to have to face Mr Wadeson," Peter said firmly.

"I may as well hand myself straight over to the magistrate and save myself the trouble of facing him," Mr Johnson said weakly.

"This is exactly why you are in this situation!" Rosalind snapped, finally losing patience with her father. "If you had just diversified or even let the business go, none of this would have happened! But no, you had to have your precious business, but who is going to buy anything from a man who kills innocents? You are ruined with far worse consequences than if you would have just accepted the change in the market."

"The business was my life," Mr Johnson said.

"Yes, that was made clear to us from a very early age. A pity your family wasn't your life, but you will reap what you have sown; not one of your children will ever want to see you again, I can promise you that!" Rosalind said. "Peter I can't demand you don't help him; you are too good a man, but don't feel under any obligation from me to try to help this fool."

Rosalind left the room, and Peter sighed. "My wife is correct; the consequences for you now are far greater than if you would have just accepted bankruptcy."

"It's easy to say that now," Mr Johnson said, "But it had all just seemed so simple at the time."

"What are you going to do?" Peter asked.

"I have no idea," Mr Johnson almost wailed.

"I suggest you return to the Crown and tell Mr Wadeson you are not going to put up with his blackmail any longer. This has to stop, Mr Johnson; standing up to him is the only way," Peter said.

"He will report what I have done," Mr Johnson said, horrified at the thought of speaking to Mr Wadeson.

"We will face that together. Frederick, Joseph and myself will all work to sort things out. You may lose your business, but the reality is that he was the one who threw the slaves overboard; you had no control over that. You will need to be honest with the authorities, including what has happened to Annabelle and hopefully there will be some sympathy towards you." Peter said, struggling himself with having any compassion towards the man. "The reality is that unless you face up to him, he will continue to take and take and take. Once you give him your business, what are you going to do then? Is he going to ask for your home? Our homes?"

Mr Johnson paled, "He has already mentioned needing a house and liking ours."

"Exactly! He will see you destitute, so you have to face up to him and suffer the consequences. They will be far preferable to dealing with him for the rest of your days," Peter said.

"I know; I will," Mr Johnson responded, but he looked dejected.

Peter wondered what he would have been like at the height of his success. His four daughters were all intelligent, capable women; they must have learned it from him in some ways. He understood how it was to be facing a future he had not anticipated, but he also knew the importance of facing what was the right thing to do, no matter how difficult it was.

*

Mr Johnson left his son-in-law and returned to the Crown. Knocking on Mr Wadeson's door was one of the hardest things he had to do. Once answered there would be no turning back.

Wadeson shouted through the door to 'come in'. He looked sharply at Mr Johnson's pale face and reluctant stance. "What's happened?" he asked, immediately on the alert.

Mr Johnson faltered and then squared his shoulders. It was time to be strong in the face of his tormentor. "Eleanor has been married with a special licence. I didn't know anything about it until this morning. Everyone knows everything that has been going on between us, and it stops here," he said, sounding braver than he felt.

"You damn fool!" Mr Wadeson spat. "I knew they would do something like this!" he jumped out of his bed and dragged his portmanteau, starting to throw his garments into it.

"Is the business not enough?" Mr Johnson asked, alarmed at what the unpredictable man would do.

"Oh, I am going to have the business, I can promise you that, and I am going to make you pay highly for this!" Mr Wadeson snarled, hurrying to dress not caring about privacy.

"You know what I have; I was giving you everything anyway," Mr Johnson bleated.

"I was to have a daughter; now you have reneged. You will make up for this; I want more funds to start with. You had better beg those stuck up relations of yours and ask them for some blunt and fast. I will be returning soon, and I want double the money I was promised."

"Double?" Mr Johnson said faintly. "My family don't want anything to do with me," he said sadly. "They are disgusted with what I've done; they won't give me anything! Where are you going?" he suddenly asked, realising that Mr Wadeson was putting on his waistcoat. His bruises still prominent making him look even more menacing in his current mood.

"Whether your family is being awkward or not is not my problem; just get the money," Mr Wadeson snapped.

"No," Mr Johnson said, swallowing with nerves as soon as he said the word.

"What?" Mr Wadeson said quietly, turning to face Mr Johnson.

"I can't go on with the lies. Do what you will; I'm not handing you my business or my money; find someone else to live off."

Mr Wadeson lashed out and sent Mr Johnson sprawling across the floor. The older man moaned, but managed to sit up, wiping his cut lip on his sleeve. "You will do exactly as I say, or I will see you hang!" Mr Wadeson said, reassured when Mr Johnson flinched at his words. "I will be returning in a few days. I expect you to have returned home and have all the paperwork in order with the additional funds I want."

"Where are you going?" Mr Johnson said, surprised he was letting him out of his sight. Mr Wadeson had been his constant shadow since he first made his demands.

"Why, I am going to show that youngest daughter of yours what happens to someone who defies me!"

Mr Johnson was never one for great shows of affection, but he did care for his daughters, albeit in a poorly judged way. The thought of his youngest daughter being faced with an angry Mr Wadeson frightened Mr Johnson to the core. He struggled to get up.

"I won't let you harm her!" he gasped, grabbing at Wadeson.

"If I didn't need the paperwork signed, I would kill you now!" Mr Wadeson spat. "Get out of my way, you fool!" He pushed Mr Johnson hard in the chest and sent him reeling into the fire grate. There was no remorse when Mr Johnson was still after impact; it just allowed Mr Wadeson to continue his plans with no further hindrance.

Before Mr Wadeson left the room, he bent over Mr Johnson and listened to his breathing. Happy the man was still alive and he would not hang for such a buffoon, he gave him a kick for good measure and left the room, keen to start his journey.

Chapter 20

Eleanor dozed in the carriage, wrapped in her husband's arms. It had been the most wonderful two days of her life, and she was happier than she had ever been. They had not been separated since being reunited at Mrs Adams's home. Her wedding had been quiet due to necessity, but she could not feel sad about what could have been, because she was married to the man she loved.

Joseph kissed the top of her head. "Wake up sleepyhead; we are nearly home."

Eleanor smiled, sitting up and reaching for her bonnet, which had been flung on the opposite seat of the carriage. "Home. That's a lovely word."

Joseph smiled. "Everyone will be anticipating your arrival. I was a confirmed bachelor when I left; they will be keen to see the woman who has stolen my heart."

Eleanor groaned. "I wish I had taken note of how Rosalind ran her home when I was with her," she said, for the first time looking a little daunted. "I'm not sure I'm quite prepared for the running of a large house."

Joseph kissed her; he sometimes forgot she was only twenty, but he was determined nothing would spoil their bliss. "My housekeeper will love you and help every step of the way, just as Peter's will have done with Rosalind, and my mother will welcome you with open arms."

"Rosalind had some experience running our own home," Eleanor explained. "Mother was involved if there were any entertainments to be planned, but Rosalind organised many of the day-to-day needs. Such things bored mother."

"Your parents really did not involve themselves in family life, did they?"

"No, they had business and looking good diverting them from the mundane aspects of life. They aren't bad people really, just indifferent," Eleanor said. She might have felt differently if Rosalind had been of a less capable character but, as it was, she never really felt they had been neglected because Rosalind had seen to it they were not.

"Well, since I'm an only child, my mother will dote on you. She had despaired that I would ever marry. Because you are such a beautiful, respectable, intelligent woman, she will immediately fall under your spell as I did," Joseph said with a smile.

Eleanor tried to suppress the fluttering of nerves she felt every time she thought of meeting Joseph's mother. She wondered what she would think of the plain daughter of a 'cit' her son was bringing home, but she was determined she was not going to voice her fears; nothing was going to mar their happiness.

The carriage eventually arrived at the Adlington estate, and Joseph handed his new bride out. Her peach dress was slightly travel weary, but still looked the exquisitely made garment it was. A cream spencer jacket covered the top of the dress, hiding for the moment, the delicate peach flowers that edged the neckline. Eleanor's bonnet was covered in cream and decorated with peach flowers and feathers. Cream gloves and boots finished off the outfit. She was the daughter of a 'cit', but dressed in a way that would have been perfectly acceptable in any Paris fashion house.

The staff were waiting for introductions as was the custom when a new family member was brought home, and Joseph introduced his slightly blushing wife to everyone. He swelled with pride at the way Eleanor spoke to everyone, taking time to listen to their answers and ask for further information. Some of the staff showed the relief that dispelled the worry the introduction of a new mistress brought. A confirmed bachelor would always make staff worry about what type of a woman would be attracted to their master. When it was a rich, handsome, titled gentlemen, not all those attracted to him would be the type to be kind to staff.

The final person to be introduced was the Dowager Duchess. She was a tall, slender lady, clearly in her early fifties. She was dressed in a deep purple taffeta; the dress was unadorned, but undoubtedly elegant. She was an attractive woman, made more so by her smile of welcome.

"You've arrived safe and sound," she smiled at her son. "It has been too long since you've been home."

"I had to chase across country to follow this one," Joseph said, smiling at Eleanor and kissing her hand. "She proved difficult to convince I was the one to marry her."

The Dowager turned to Eleanor. "You are very welcome here, my dear. I'm looking forward to getting to know you; Joseph's letters have been full of you."

"Thank you, I'm very happy to be here," Eleanor responded with a smile and a curtsey.

"Not as happy as I am," Joseph whispered, once again kissing her hand. He could not shock the staff and his mother by grabbing his wife and kissing her on the lips, but he also could not stop himself from touching her in some way.

"Come in, come in, I want to know all about you," the Dowager Duchess said, stepping inside, so everyone could enter the Adlington household. She led the travellers into the saloon where she served tea and asked Eleanor about her family and history. There was not the condemnation of her background Eleanor had feared, and she started to relax.

After they drank enough tea to satisfy even the thirstiest, Eleanor was shown to her chamber to change for their evening meal. It was a large room decorated in golds, making it a warm, bright space. When she was shown around the house, the Dowager Duchess had been at pains to say she should change whatever she wished to make the house her own. Eleanor was relieved her new mother seemed to welcome her into the household without any hesitation; it was the final cause of worry that could now be put to one side, and she could relax completely. Only a few days ago she had thought she would never get through the future she was facing, but now she was perfectly happy.

*

A small knock on the door revealed Joseph, walking into the room with a smile on his face. Eleanor immediately dismissed her maid; she already knew the expression that promised of untold pleasure to come.

"Do you like our room?" Joseph asked, wrapping his arms around his wife and not giving her the opportunity to respond as his lips met hers as soon as he had uttered the words.

Eventually Eleanor pulled away. "Our room?" she asked with a raised eyebrow, not quite able to stop the smile reaching her lips.

"Yes, I decided at Sudworth Hall I really liked sleeping with you," Joseph explained. "And so I thought we should continue here; I've told the housekeeper I will only be using my dressing room."

"So, you are being masterful and not giving me a choice in the matter, are you?" Eleanor asked.

"As I spend most of my time near you being nothing but a weak fool, willing to do anything to make you happy, I need to take advantage and be masterful when I can," Joseph said, his eyes sparkling at Eleanor.

"When you put it like that, how can I object?" Eleanor said, leaning in to kiss him. She wondered if she would ever get tired of touching him, because she could not resist at the moment.

Joseph groaned and pulled her dress off her shoulders. "I think you should delay dressing," he muttered, making her step out of the pooled material.

"What about your mother?" Eleanor asked.

"I'm sure she can wait a little longer for food," Joseph whispered, before lifting Eleanor and carrying her to their bed.

*

Peter had received a message from the inn to say there had been an accident. He immediately rode out accompanied by Rosalind, who had insisted on joining him.

They were shown into the room where Mr Johnson had been laid on his bed. He looked a deathly shade of grey, and sported a large lump to his head. "He had a fall your Grace; we heard the shouting in Mr Wadeson's room, but when Mr Wadeson stormed out there was no sign of Mr Johnson. I thought it prudent to check, and he was on the floor unconscious," the apologetic innkeeper explained. "We've sent for the doctor."

"Thank you," Peter responded. The innkeeper left the pair alone, shutting the door behind him.

Rosalind paled at the state of her father. She approached the bed. "I may be disgusted with everything he has done, but I didn't wish him dead," she said to Peter.

"I know. Let's wait to see what the doctor says," Peter said gently. It was obvious Mr Wadeson was worse than they had imagined; it did appear Mr Johnson had been left for dead.

"Father? Can you hear me?" Rosalind asked, bending so her mouth was near his ear. "What happened? As if we need to ask!"

Mr Johnson groaned, and his eyes fluttered; every movement seemed to cost him a great deal, but Rosalind saw he was determined to speak, she moved even closer to him. "Eleanor," Mr Johnson muttered.

"Eleanor?" Rosalind asked in surprise. "Father, she is married. You aren't still hoping she's going to marry Mr Wadeson are you?"

Mr Johnson moaned again. "Eleanor!" he said, but this time there was an urgency to his voice. The effort seemed to exhaust him, and he closed his eyes.

"Perhaps he thinks I am Eleanor?" Rosalind suggested a little confused.

"No, I think it's something else," Peter said with a firm set to his lips. "Let me try." He moved to stand by Mr Johnson and touched him gently on his shoulder. "Mr Johnson, are you trying to tell us something about Eleanor?"

Mr Johnson moved his head slightly, he winced in pain, but the nod had been in the affirmative.

Peter glanced at Rosalind, before continuing. "Is Eleanor in danger from Mr Wadeson?" he asked.

Again, the nod came, and Rosalind gasped for breath. "How? Surely he won't find them?" she asked Peter, panicked.

"I don't honestly know if they have gone on a wedding trip or returned to his estate. I thought it prudent not to know; the fewer people know the better," Peter said to Rosalind.

"Eleanor!" Mr Johnson groaned again.

"What shall we do? He is agitated enough for me to think he took the threat, whatever it is, seriously," Rosalind said.

"If they have gone on a trip, they will be safely tucked out of the way, somewhere distant I hope; but if they have returned to his estate, it won't take Wadeson long to find out where it is," Peter voiced fears they were both thinking.

"We need to send word," Rosalind said, torn between needing to care for her father and warn her youngest sister.

"Rosalind, you stay here until the doctor arrives. If we have to move him to Sudworth Hall we will; just find out whatever is needed to care for him, and it will be done. I'm going to send an express message to Joseph; if he's not at his estate, they may have heard where they are staying and forward my message on," Peter instructed, starting to leave the room.

"Peter!" Rosalind said, making her husband pause in the doorway. "Will she be safe?"

"Adlington is a decent man, and he adores Eleanor," Peter said gently. "He will defend her whatever the cost to himself."

Rosalind nodded, and Peter left the room.

*

Eleanor sat opposite the Dowager Duchess. Joseph left them together, saying he needed to spend time with his steward. It was the first time the two women had been left alone together.

"Are you intending staying in the area, or does London call?" the Dowager Duchess asked, accepting a refilled cup of tea from Eleanor.

"No, you will find us both content to stay here for the foreseeable future," Eleanor replied. "I think we are both ready to stay in one place; we've both been travelling for differing reasons. It will be pleasant to spend a period of time without the need to plan for the next trip."

"I'm glad to hear those words, but I don't want our Society to be too tedious for you," the Dowager responded.

"Not at all; there is a lot to be said for a quiet life!" Eleanor said with feeling.

"I've longed for Joseph to return home, but London or Brighton always seemed to have a bigger pull; he seems less restless this time though. I think it is the first time he has not walked around here with a constant frown on his face."

"Oh?" Eleanor replied, surprised at the words. "He has spoken warmly of his home."

"I'm glad to hear that; a young man doesn't always wish to be at home, especially when his mother is constantly reminding him he needs to marry," the Dowager said with a smile.

"Well, he listened," Eleanor responded with a slight blush.

"I'm glad." The Dowager was prevented from further conversation by a coughing fit that lasted some minutes. Eleanor had moved to sit next to the Dowager and rubbed her back in an effort to relieve the coughing.

When the Dowager's handkerchief was moved from her mouth, Eleanor was horrified to see blood on the material. "Let me send for the doctor; you are ill," Eleanor said.

"No, no," the Dowager responded, her voice quiet due to the effects of the coughing. "Just let me have some tea; I'll be fine."

Eleanor held a cup to the Dowager's lips and fed her the drink as she wanted it. Only when she received a small smile did she move the cup, but returned to sit next to the Dowager. "You are obviously in need of a doctor," she said gently.

"I have seen more doctors than I ever want to see again," came the sad smile of the Dowager as she patted Eleanor's hand. "There is nothing to be done for consumption. I have been lucky to have lived to see Joseph married; it was my only wish to see him settled. It's hard for a mother to leave her only child alone in the world, but now I don't need to worry; he has you, and already I have seen how much he cares for you in the way he looks at you."

Eleanor blushed at the compliment. "He isn't alone and won't ever be in the future, but please don't say there is no hope, I've only just met you!"

The Dowager laughed at Eleanor's words. "I hope not to be dying for a little while yet," she said, her voice gaining its normal strength as her breathing became easier.

"Good." Eleanor said firmly. "Now I need to know everything about the disease and what I need to do to help you. I have just gained a mother; I'm not giving her up so easily!"

Eleanor's kind words were to comfort the Dowager far more than she could have realised. Knowing her son was loved was one thing, but knowing her new daughter-in-law was keen to care for her old and ailing self released some of the tension the Dowager Duchess had been feeling. She did not wish her son to see some of the things she would have to go through as the end neared, but she hoped after Eleanor's words she would find someone who cared enough to help when needed.

*

Joseph sought his mother out when morning visits ended. The Dowager Duchess always needed a lie down to recover from the strain of visits. He did not wish for Eleanor to hear the conversation he needed to have, at least until after he sought his mother's advice.

He knocked on the door around the time the Dowager would be rising, hopefully refreshed from her sleep. Joseph opened the door when called and popped his head through the opening. "Have you a few minutes to spare your favourite son?" he asked, his eyes twinkling.

"I always have time for my only son," came the amused reply. The Dowager lay back against her pillows and patted the bed beside her; she always had time for her boy.

"You know how to wound your son," Joseph said. He walked across to his mother after closing the door behind him and kissed her forehead before sitting down on the stool of her dressing table. "I need your advice," he said becoming serious.

"What is it?" she asked, immediately alert.

"I didn't want to tell you about the background to my marriage," Joseph started. "But I'm afraid I've received a letter, and it forces me to do so."

"You'd better explain."

Joseph told his mother all about his first meetings with Eleanor in Bath and in what way they had separated. He was completely honest about his own behaviour and cruel words; there was the need to be truthful about the situation. He then went on to explain how he had chased Eleanor to the Duke of Sudworth's house and the story around her father and Mr Wadeson.

He had reached the elopement and special licence when he paused to laugh. "This story must sound horrific to your ears! It sounds bad enough to mine, and I was a willing participant!" he said with a shake of his head.

"It has certainly been an adventure for you both, and I am glad you sorted things out. Even on such a short acquaintance with Eleanor, I can see she is a perfect match for you," the Dowager said. She would mull over the details later; for now, there was obviously something amiss that was yet to be mentioned.

"I think so too," Joseph smiled before becoming serious once more. "I had hoped it would be the end of it, but I've received an urgent message from Peter, and I'm not sure what to do about it."

"Tell me," came the reassuring response.

"Apparently it got very ugly between Mr Wadeson and Mr Johnson. It seems that even now it is not known whether the injuries Mr Johnson received will be fatal or not, but Mr Wadeson had set-off determined to find Eleanor," Joseph said.

"I see. This man isn't going to be open to reason is he?" the Dowager asked.

"No. He thinks he has been cheated by Mr Johnson, and myself as well, I suppose, and has set-out to get what he believes to be his," Joseph said. "I don't want to be overdramatic, but I think Eleanor may be in some danger from him."

"It is wise to think that, but she will be safe here," the Dowager reassured him.

"I'm not sure whether to tell Eleanor or not," Joseph pondered.

"Not at this time," his mother replied. "I do think the key staff should be told. Between us we can make sure she is never left alone, and we can arrange to hire more men to patrol the gardens day and night, challenging anyone who enters."

"Do you think that would be enough?" Joseph asked. "I feel like I want to lock her into a secure cell where he can't reach her until we find him."

The Dowager smiled. "I think that's a little unnecessary, but I understand your sentiments. We will protect her, but I don't wish to worry her; let her continue to settle in. I would hate her to feel insecure here."

"Yes, you are right. This is her home, and I don't want to upset her, but I will start carrying my pistols everywhere when we venture out of doors," Joseph said firmly.

"I don't want you putting yourself in harm's way," the Dowager said quickly.

Joseph smiled. "I promise I won't be foolish, but I will do anything I can to protect her."

"I know, and I would expect nothing else from my fine son," came the quiet reply.

"Now I've worried you!" Joseph cursed himself.

"I've been worried about you since the day you were born, and it will not stop until my last breath. It is a mother's role to worry, but we will face this together," the Dowager said firmly. "Now go to your wife, and I will inform the staff."

Joseph moved and kissed his mother's head. "Thank you," he whispered, before leaving her alone.

The Dowager Duchess moved to her dressing table and sat facing the mirror. She looked at her reflection. She would be eternally glad Joseph trusted her enough to confide in her, but she felt as if she had aged in the last hour. Moments passed while thoughts raced through her head and then she sat up straighter. She was the Dowager Duchess of Adlington, and no one—especially a scoundrel as had been described to her—would harm anyone dear to her; of that she was sure. She moved to ring the bell to summon the housekeeper and butler: there was much to arrange.

Chapter 21

Two weeks into being at her new home, and Eleanor was beginning to feel as if she belonged. She appreciated the help the Dowager had given in instructing a large household and planning ahead. Now though, she met with cook and the housekeeper without the support of the Dowager and, although she still had a lot to learn, she was feeling more at ease in the role.

She had heard that her father was not well but had not been told the reasons. Joseph had sent a message through to ask that unless it was necessary Eleanor should not be told. Rosalind wrote to say Mr Johnson had suffered a fall and although he was not recovered there was no deterioration in his condition.

Eleanor joined the Dowager Duchess in the drawing room for afternoon tea. She had been sorting through the attics with the housekeeper, but now she was ready for a refreshing drink.

The Dowager smiled as Eleanor entered the room. "Do I need to apologise for the amount stored in the attics?"

Eleanor laughed, "I think it will take us at least a week to itemise everything."

"That's a yes then!" the Dowager smiled. "I'm sorry; I should have gone through them years ago, but I never had half the energy you have."

"You have had a bad chest for years; I'm glad you didn't venture up there; the dust was horrifying to Mrs Manning," Eleanor said of the long-serving housekeeper.

"She'll probably have an army of maids up there before you next venture into them," the Dowager said with a laugh.

"She did mention something along those lines, but I told her not to fret," Eleanor said.

"She may not listen."

"I didn't think she would; something about her frown every time we touched anything was the clue she wasn't reassured by my words," Eleanor said.

The floor to ceiling windows were open to let the breeze and sunshine into the room, and Eleanor smiled when Joseph walked through them. "I knew I would find you both lazing around," he said with a smile, placing a kiss on Eleanor's cheek.

"Shall I pour you a cup of tea, my hardworking husband?" Eleanor said with a smirk.

"Of course, at least I have earned my rest," Joseph said, leaning back on the sofa.

"She has worked hard all morning!" his mother tsked at him. "Don't you start criticising my daughter!"

"That's all I need: two women to berate me," Joseph said with a lazy smile.

"In that case, let me take one of them off your hands," came the deep drawl from the open window.

All three of the party jumped at the voice. Joseph stood, shielding Eleanor. "How the hell did you get through the patrols in the parkland?" Joseph ground out.

"Patrols?" Eleanor said, standing next to Joseph. Her face was pale; the colour had drained the moment she had seen Mr Wadeson, but she felt less vulnerable now that she was married and next to Joseph.

"Yes, your loving husband has been keeping his parkland full of men, searching for me. I'm actually quite flattered," Mr Wadeson sneered. He was holding two pistols, and a third was sticking out of the waistband of his breeches. All three in the party were watching the pistols he held.

"Joseph?" Eleanor asked.

"Peter wrote to say Mr Wadeson was on our trail, but I didn't want to worry you," Joseph explained quickly, wanting to concentrate on working out a way that would see the removal of his wife and mother from the room.

"So, that's why I've never been left alone!" Eleanor said with the dawning realisation of being followed for the last two weeks. "I wish you would have said; I just put it down to you having overly attentive staff. I must say I'm quite embarrassed; I shall have to apologise to some of them later: I've been quite sharp sometimes!"

Joseph laughed and gave Eleanor a sidelong look and a shrug; not knowing whether to be shocked or amused that his wife was taking him to task while they were both facing a gunman. "Sorry, I thought it was best; they'll understand."

"I jolly well hope so," Eleanor huffed.

"Brave to the last," Mr Wadeson said. "Now I haven't got all day; Eleanor come with me, and we can finish all this."

"She is going nowhere," Joseph snarled, all amusement gone.

"Says the man who isn't armed, while I have two pistols, one for the Duke, one for the old woman," Mr Wadeson said with a sickly smile.

"No!" Eleanor said quickly. "There is no need for anyone to get hurt on my account; I will come without a fight as long as you don't use the pistols."

"Eleanor, there is no way I'm letting you leave with him," Joseph said through gritted teeth. "We know what a monster he is."

"And there is no way I'm going to be responsible for the injury or death of you or your mother," Eleanor ground back.

"Ah, marital bliss; it is a delight to see," Mr Wadeson mocked.

"Oh, shut up you little weasel!" Eleanor snapped. "In fact that is an insult to weasels! You are a parasite, nothing more. You tried to bleed my father dry, and now you are threatening to shoot us. What next?"

"You'll find out soon enough, Duchess," Mr Wadeson spat, "And believe me: I'll make sure it's something you will not be able to forget in a hurry."

"She isn't going anywhere with you," Joseph said, stepping in front of Eleanor.

"I can't decide if you are brave or stupid," Mr Wadeson said before firing the first pistol.

Eleanor and the Dowager screamed as Joseph was knocked over the chair he had been standing in front of from the force of the shot. Eleanor was at Joseph's side in a blink of an eye, calling out his name. "Oh, my god! Oh, my god!" she repeated.

Joseph held his shoulder and looked up at his wife. "It's a flesh wound; don't worry I'll live," he whispered. "Eleanor, whatever you do, don't go with him."

"I can't risk you; I can't Joseph," Eleanor cried, tears streaming down her face. "I would rather be shot."

"No, Eleanor, please," Joseph grunted as he tried to sit up. He looked at Wadeson. "I'll give you anything you want: name your price."

Mr Wadeson smiled. "That's better, respect at last. By the way, just for the record, I aimed at your arm; if I'd wanted to kill you outright, I would have done. I am an excellent shot. Duchess, lock the door."

The drawing room door was being opened gently. Eleanor could see the pistol the butler was holding, but shook her head at him. No one was getting shot on her account. "Please close the door, Benson," she instructed firmly. The butler looked at her, but she nodded gently in reassurance, and he withdrew. "No one will disturb us now," she said turning back to Mr Wadeson.

"Name your price," Joseph said through gritted teeth. It might be only a flesh wound, but it hurt like hell.

"You see, therein lies the problem," Mr Wadeson said, seeming to ponder the proposal. "I could ask for money, but I've got quite a bit squirreled away; Mr Johnson's businesses weren't doing quite as bad as he thought, so really I have more than my needs. I could ask for property, but I've always been one to travel around, looking for the next fool. You see, it comes down to this: the only thing I want is your wife and, at this moment in time, it looks like I'm going to get her."

"If I could interrupt?" the Dowager Duchess said, standing tall in front of the unlit fireplace. "We have never met before, but I am the mother of the man you have just shot."

"I guessed," Mr Wadeson said rudely.

"I thought you might have," she said as if it were the most natural conversation in the world. "He is my only son, so I am quite protective of him."

"Tell him to hand over his wife and then you can have him all to yourself," Mr Wadeson sneered.

"There is a little problem with that," the Dowager continued. "You see, I find there are two points I disagree with you about. The first is I actually quite like Eleanor and would like her to stay, and the second point is I believe once you have Eleanor, my son will still not be safe. You have two loaded pistols at your disposal Mr Wadeson; is that one for me, one for my son?"

"If you don't stop talking, it could well be," Mr Wadeson said in disgust.

"Ah, I see; so you wish me to come to my conclusion?" the Dowager continued.

"Yes, woman, hurry up!" Mr Wadeson snapped.

"As you wish," the Dowager seemed to shrug, but she brought her hands round to her front, instead of holding them behind her back as she had been the whole time Mr Wadeson had been in the room. In her hands was the glint of two small pistols. Mr Wadeson acted quickly, moving his hand from pointing at Joseph, but the Dowager was ahead of him and shot both pistols simultaneously. The force of the shots knocked Mr Wadeson off his feet; the pistol he still had in his hand went off, but the bullet hit the coving, causing no damage to anyone in the room.

Eleanor flung herself at the Dowager and dragged her to the floor, expecting Mr Wadeson to aim with his third pistol, but there was no movement. "Are you hurt?" Eleanor asked, not realising the shot had hit the ceiling.

"I'm fine, but Mr Wadeson won't be. I, too, am an excellent shot and both bullets will have gone through his heart. I think I may need to explain myself to the magistrate," the Dowager said with a shaky laugh.

Joseph stood and walked over to where the body lay. He took some pleasure in seeing the look of surprise on the dead man's face before he looked at his wife and mother. "Dead," he said. "I could do with some brandy."

Joseph's words stirred Eleanor into action; she ran to the door, allowing in the staff gathered in the hall. In what seemed like a matter of minutes the family had been moved to the morning room, the doctor and magistrate had been called for and brandy had been handed round to staff as well as family.

After Joseph's wound had been treated and his arm secured in a sling, the magistrate spoke to all involved, and the house resumed a little more of an air of normality. The drawing room was cleaned and, although it would be some time before the coving was replaced, there was no other outward sign of what had happened some hours earlier.

After the staff served the evening meal and the family were together in the drawing room, Joseph, wearing a sling that had both women fussing over him, they finally spoke of what had happened.

"I wish you had told me," Eleanor said.

"I didn't want to worry you; I want this to feel like it is your home not a place sullied with fear caused by him," Joseph said.

Eleanor smiled. "My home is wherever you are, no matter where that is."

"That my dear, was the correct response to give," the Dowager beamed at Eleanor.

Eleanor looked at the Dowager and tried to frown at her. "Don't think you get away so lightly; you obviously knew about it and didn't tell me either."

"I was carrying out my son's wishes," the Dowager said loftily.

"For once," Joseph muttered, making his mother smile. "I do want to know where you stored those pistols though."

"From the moment you told me of the threat, I've been carrying them round with me. I've only worn dresses that have two pockets; it has been quite restrictive, I'll have you know," the Dowager responded.

"You've been armed for two weeks?" Joseph asked in astonishment.

"Yes, one thing your father taught me in our younger days was how to be a good shot. He used to tease me and say if we ever had a revolution here, at least I would be able to shoot my way out of trouble," the Dowager said with a smile.

"If Mr Wadeson had seen you before you'd had time to shoot…." Eleanor said with a shudder.

"He was too intent on you two; I was just the unfortunate extra in the room. I could see he was going to kill Joseph; we all knew it was going to be the only way to stop him pursuing you," the Dowager said, becoming serious. "I could not let that happen."

"Well, Eleanor, I think we're safe in the knowledge that, whatever happens in the future, we will be safe; no highwaymen or robbers will scare us, not while mother is around!" Joseph said, proud of his mother's calm way of dealing with the situation but also relieved the two women in his life were not hurt.

"I used to think Rosalind was scary, but she was never armed; remind me never to argue with your mother!" Eleanor said with feeling.

"I shall remind you of those words," the Dowager replied with a smile. "I feel my remaining years are going to be very enjoyable."

"Eleanor, what have you said? We're doomed!" Joseph said dramatically, before being hit by a cushion thrown expertly by the Dowager Duchess.

Epilogue

Frederick, Lord Stannage, paced the drawing room floor. "Why does it take so long?" he ground out, to no one in particular of the gathered family.

Peter, Duke of Sudworth handed Frederick a glass. "Have this: it will calm your nerves," he said gently. His own first born was less than a year old, so he was fully aware of the feelings of the expectant father.

"How do people go through this more than once? We are going to only have one child; she can't go through this again!" Frederick muttered.

Peter smiled at his wife Rosalind, who blushed slightly before looking away. She was increasing again, but it was very early, so no one knew apart from the husband and wife. "I suppose you just pray for them to be taken care of. Annabelle is strong and healthy; she will be fine, I'm sure of it."

Frederick looked at Peter and sighed in an effort to calm himself. He was in his own home, Stannage House, surrounded by Annabelle's family. He cursed himself; her two younger sisters were both showing signs of their rounding bellies as the babies inside them grew. That is what comes of all marrying within a year of each other, he mused to himself.

"I'm sorry," Frederick said to Eleanor and Grace; he did not wish to alarm them.

"Don't worry; it is a reassurance to know this is exactly how Harry and Joseph will be: it means we won't be suffering alone," Eleanor said with a smile at her husband.

Frederick recommenced his pacing, and Rosalind joined her two sisters. "I received a letter from Mother yesterday."

"Is she well?" Grace asked.

"She's her usual self," Rosalind said with a grimace. "She didn't ask after any of us, just filled the letter with what she was doing."

Since their father died by catching a fever a few months after his accident, which he was just too weak to shake off, all his business interests had been sold. The four daughter's had insisted the money raised should go to recompense the families of the slaves that had been drowned. Peter and Frederick worked together to trace the villages that had been attacked by the crew members and sent envoys over to provide funds for the families.

Grace and Eleanor received their dowries even though both had expressed strongly they had not wanted the money. Rosalind insisted they should have it especially as their father had saved the money at a time when he was not involved in illegal activity. Both sisters decided to settle the dowries on their children.

Their mother had not been pleased that what she considered to be her money was being distributed in such a way, but Peter, normally the gentle one, had quite firmly said if she did not agree to his terms, he would go to the authorities and inform them of everything illegal that had happened. Mrs Johnson had said he would not dare, but when Peter had listed the scandals he had had to deal with in the public eye, she backed down; there was no doubt that Peter would not shy away from a last scandal that would actually only show herself and her husband in a poor light.

Mrs Johnson had decided a home in Italy would be preferable to remaining in England. She would not miss her daughters and had little interest in the fact that she was becoming a grandmother; in fact it added an extra incentive to leave the country rather than stay.

The party in the drawing room was interrupted by the arrival of Frederick's elder sister, Caroline and her husband Harold. "I believe our timing is fortuitous?" Caroline asked with a smile at her pale-faced brother.

"Caroline, it has been hours!" Frederick said, hugging his sister to him.

"She will be well," Caroline whispered to him. "Oh, Freddy, you are to be a Papa!" The older sister whispered tearfully to her brother.

"Don't Caroline," Frederick said with a smile. "Or you will see me blubbering like a child."

"My Lord?" the voice of the butler interrupted the brother and sister. "The nurse has sent word to say you have a daughter, and her Ladyship would like to see you."

"A daughter?" Frederick said, sitting down.

"Yes, a beautiful daughter," Caroline said with a choke to her voice. "Freddy, Annabelle wants to see you."

"Of course," Frederick said, rising as if in a trace.

"I think, I'd better accompany you," Caroline said with a smile and guided her brother out of the room.

They knocked on Annabelle's chamber door, and the nurse opened it, stepping outside with a bundle in her arms. "Here she is, my Lord," she said, passing Frederick the bundle.

"My wife?" Frederick asked.

"Her Ladyship is still a little uncomfortable, so we will get her settled and then you can see her," the nurse explained.

Further talking was interrupted by a scream of pain from the bedchamber. Frederick paled at the sound being wrenched from his wife's lips.

The nurse opened the door; Frederick and Caroline saw the pained face of Annabelle as she looked for the nurse. "Nurse, the pains are coming back!" she moaned, her head falling back.

"Nurse?" Frederick asked, panicked.

"All will be well, my Lord," the nurse said, before firmly closing the door behind her.

Caroline gently took her niece from Frederick's arms; he looked as if he did not realise he held her "Frederick, the nurse knows what she is doing."

"What if I lose her, Caroline?" Frederick said, turning to his sister. She had seen her brother hurt over the years; because of his mismatched eyes, he had been hurt more times than she cared to remember, but nothing compared to the look of fear on his face.

"Freddy, let's leave the nurse to her job and take this beautiful girl to the rest of her family," Caroline said firmly.

They opened the drawing room door and were immediately surrounded by the new arrival's other aunties. Rosalind looked at Frederick's face in question. "Annabelle?" she asked. Peter had not left her side after she had delivered her child; she was surprised at Frederick's appearance.

"Something's not right," Frederick said dully.

The room silenced at his words, and all sat down. Caroline never left Frederick's side, but the Johnson girls had returned to the sides of their husbands, needing their comfort when their sister was so obviously not recovering from childbirth as expected.

All seemed to focus on the ticking of the grandfather clock in the room, while listening out for footsteps that would herald the coming of news. An hour had passed until the drawing room door opened, and the butler reappeared.

"My Lord, the nurse is ready to see you now."

Frederick turned to Caroline, who stood up immediately. "We will go together," his sister said, holding her niece close to her heart. The pair left the room, while the remaining occupants seemed to huddle even closer to the person they were next to.

Frederick was led into the bedchamber, and the nurse bustled up to him. "I told you there was nothing to worry about," she tsked at Frederick's worried face. "Lady Stannage just had a little surprise for us," she said, leading the way over to the bed.

"Annabelle?" Frederick whispered, hardly believing Annabelle was looking at him, although she looked exhausted and pale.

Annabelle smiled a weary but happy smile at her husband and reached out her hand to him. "I will be well, Freddy," she whispered. "It seems there was a little problem."

"But you are well now?" Frederick asked.

"I am, but we have taken on more than we thought," Annabelle said and gestured to the bundle in her arms. "Our little girl has a sister."

"A sister?" Frederick asked, stupidly.

"Yes, two babies," Annabelle said with a smile.

Frederick sank on the chair the nurse had placed near him. "Two? But how…?"

"I don't think we should start embarrassing the staff by explaining how, do you?" Annabelle teased, welcoming her first born daughter back into her arms.

Annabelle's words seemed to do the trick, and Frederick roused himself a little. "Two girls: I'm going to be surrounded by females!" he said, for the first time a wide smile emerging. Frederick paused and looked at Annabelle and the nurse. "Their eyes?"

"Freddy, I asked your mother when she could tell that something was different, and she said from the moment you were born the difference was clear. They did not know how it would look as you grew; the green wasn't green from birth, but there was a mismatch in the eyes. Neither of your daughters has that," Annabelle said quietly, knowing he would not wish the oddity to be passed down to his children.

"You're sure?" Frederick asked.

"Yes, we don't know about in the future, but whatever happens they're going to have enough cousins to protect them if needed. All you need to worry about is what names we are going to choose for two girls!"

"It was hard enough choosing one name, never mind two!" Frederick said, finally relaxing and realising his worries, for now, were over.

Annabelle reached for his hand. "I am so very, very glad I met you, Lord Stannage. I love you." She did not care that they still had three members of staff in the room; she would love her husband until her dying day, and she wanted everyone to know it.

*

Annabelle had not underestimated that her two daughters would be surrounded by cousins. Grace and Harry were to be blessed with six boys. Grace was adored by all her little men as she called them, even though every one of them took after their father in towering over their dainty mother. Harry had seven willing workers, helping him to make the gardens beautiful and his job easier. The staff that had known the reticent Harry Long, could never tire of expressing how much he had changed for the better, singing as he worked and smiling, but his look was never as gentle as the smiles he saved for his wife.

Rosalind and Peter had three children, two boys and a girl, who spent as much of their time at the gardener's cottage with Harry and Grace as they did at home. Rosalind loved that there was a steady stream of children and visitors to Sudworth Hall. They would always shock some in the locality because of their 'common' ways, but for Rosalind her home was happy, bursting with love, and that was all she had ever wished for. Annie was a part of their lives until she passed away during her fortieth year. Everyone mourned her loss, but Rosalind and Peter took comfort in knowing that, overall, she had had a good life and was loved by those who took the trouble to know her.

Eleanor and her Joseph might have lived a day's travel away, but it did not mean they were ever separated for long; hardly a sen' night passed without a visit from the Duke and Duchess of Adlington and their six children. Four girls and two boys filled Eleanor and Joseph's life. The Dowager Duchess lived to see two of her grandchildren and died a happy woman, still thanking the day Joseph brought home his new wife.

Annabelle and Frederick eventually had eight children, despite Frederick's protestations that Annabelle was not going to have another child after their first experience. None of the husbands ever got used to the waiting involved, but Frederick seemed to suffer the most. He was destined to be surrounded by females, the first six children being girls. At Annabelle's final confinement, twins appeared again, this time boys. Annabelle declared she hoped it did not mean that four boys were to follow, but she was to be spared; no other babies came along, and their family was complete with none of the children having the mismatched eyes of their father.

Frederick found that he no longer bothered about the outside world. Having odd eyes did not matter when you belonged to such a large family. As the family grew, social gatherings were filled with so many relations no one would dare to ridicule the Lord with the green and blue eyes.

Frances, Stuart and Mrs Adams were regular visitors to the family. Frances was a good friend to all the Johnson girls, and Mrs Adams was an adopted grandmother. Frances had two children, who were completely spoiled by their grandmother. Stuart was to become tutor to the boys at Sudworth Hall, continuing the job he loved with the people he thought highly of. Mrs Adams spent less time out in company; she had finally found a group of people who entertained, respected and stood up to her, and she did not need to put up with any of the nonsense she had borne over the years. So, when their parents told them of the things Mrs Adams had done before they were born, the children of the Johnson family looked at the sweet but mischievous old lady and did not believe a word said.

Many years later, the Duke of Sudworth was hosting a celebration of his youngest child and, as the party was in full swing, he held back on the edge on the dance floor. The room was swarming with his immediate and wider family. He remembered back to his wedding day, the farce of the day, meeting his bride for only the second time, each barely able to look at the other. He would never be able to believe how, from such a shaky start, such happiness and contentment could develop. All because of one man's obsession with getting a titled husband for each of his four daughters.

Sometimes, from the shakiest start, something wonderful can emerge, and the family before him was a testament to that; he smiled at his wife across the ballroom. She might be greying now, but she was still as beautiful to him as she had been on that first day. She had saved the heritage that was now their own and had given him such love over the years he would always thank the day when he had been told of a 'cit's' daughter who needed a titled husband.

*

Lady Joan does not deserve her own story, but some readers may wish to know what kind of man was attracted to her. Please read on if you do.

Lady Joan

Joan scowled to herself, giving anyone unfortunate enough to see her expression clear warning they were to give her a wide birth. She had been on the ship now for three weeks, and it was as if she were being taunted by some greater being: a storm had developed just as they were approaching port, and the ship had to stay out in open water for the safety of the vessel and the people onboard.

The journey had been bad enough: the ship earned its money by transporting cargo; the few passengers it carried just supplemented the income of the Captain and crew. Joan had never been looked after so poorly in all her days; the staff allocated to care for the paying guests would not have lasted two minutes in the service of Lord and Lady Kettering.

As if the poor service, cramped conditions and tedious journey were not enough, Joan had another cross to bear: the blasted Captain of the ship itself. He was always so damned cheerful, and he seemed to get pleasure out of seeking out Joan and talking with her, or trying to; she gave him every set-down she had ever thought of, but it seemed to only make him laugh louder.

She stared over the rail. She was not supposed to be outside in rough weather, but she could not stand to stay inside any longer. The other passengers, as well as being the most boring people in the world, were not good travellers, and she did not wish to be anywhere near the sounds or smells.

Joan looked out over the turbulent sea; there was a gap in the clouds and, over the last half hour, there seemed to be a slowing of the waves battering the ship. She sighed; she could see the island she would be calling home and even at a distance its differences were clear. There had been cruel words on both sides between herself and her mother before she had been forced to leave all she had known. Her weak father had just supported her mother in all she had said and done.

They had been very clear: she could not return home; she would be ruined because they were taking in her bastard child, and there would be too many people willing to make the connections that would show she had been stupid to the highest degree.

The problem was, she could hate Robert, the tenth Duke of Sudworth, but he had made her feel special for a little time at least. She had loved him. She had wanted to marry him since she was a young child; whether it was the title or the man she loved, she was not sure in her own mind, but it was irrelevant: he had obviously not loved her. He had abandoned her and her with child. Her parents were not aware Robert had known she was increasing before he left for Europe never to return. She could not tell anyone because of the shame she felt. He had openly laughed at her, telling her she was foolish if she thought that would tie him to her.

For the first and only time in her life, Joan had begged him to stay, but he had pushed her away and walked away from her and his home. He could not have even made false promises; she had lied to her family when she said Robert had promised to marry her: he had taken her innocence and refused to act in the only way that would not ruin her.

It was ironic now that she had started the lies that would protect her but, because of them, she would never be able to return home. She was still using her title, but she had also told anyone she deemed needed to know that she was a widow, her family name being Gilbert; that way at least she got to use Robert's name.

"Mrs Gilbert, you know I don't like my passengers out on deck when there is any danger of them being washed overboard; losing passengers isn't good for trade," came the voice of the man she wished had captained any other ship, but this one.

"My name is Lady Joan, and it is settling now," Joan said sharply. It had been a running argument for three weeks that he used her 'married' name, and she insisted he use her title.

Captain Murphy came and stood by her, holding the wooden railing in his large hands. "Aye, it is easing; we'll be docked in a few hours. There's nothing like the beauty of a storm to remind you just how small you are in comparison with the ocean," he said, looking out over the waves.

Joan looked at him sharply. He was a tall man, having to stoop when he went into the body of the ship, but Joan reached past his shoulder. She was completely opposite him in build: he was broad and strong; she had seen him grapple with the sails alongside his men, using his strength to tame the rogue pieces of canvas. They must look odd standing together, her thin with sharp features, him burly with rounded ones.

She shook her head at his description. "You can refer to this grey mass as beautiful?" she asked incredulously.

"You don't see it?" Captain Murphy asked in surprise. "Why, look at all the colours in the water: there aren't just grey; look at how the sea moves when it's angry, lashing out, but there is power and strength behind the waves that is normally hidden in the calmer waters. Yes, I think it's beautiful. It's like an angry woman, whose promise of what lies beneath the anger is ever so appealing." His eyes crinkled as his ruddy face turned to smile at her. The smile grew wider when he saw the flush that was not caused by the blustery wind.

Lady Joan stiffened at his words; she had the distinct impression he was making a joke of her. "Some see class as anger because they can't understand how to remain in their own sphere," she snapped, trying to give him a put down that would stop him constantly seeking her out. Although to be fair, she had been trying the whole of the three weeks she had been on board, and it had not worked so far.

Captain Murphy chuckled; it was deep and genuine. "Oh, Mrs Gilbert, you have been an absolute delight on this journey; I shall be sorry to see you go. You wouldn't like to stay on board would you?"

"I most certainly would not!" Joan snapped. "What kind of a doxy do you take me for?" she asked.

"Someone with your pedigree, that you have reminded me of every day these past three weeks, could never be seen as a doxy," Captain Murphy teased. "It was a respectable offer, Mrs Gilbert."

"It's Lady Joan!" Joan ground out.

"Why don't you wish to use your dead husband's name? Were you ashamed of him?" Captain Murphy became serious for once.

Joan was lost for words for a moment, but then decided that a lie is always better wrapped up in some truth. "No, I wasn't ashamed of him; I loved him, but he did not care for me," she said, some of the pain at Robert's rejection, showing in her expression.

"Well, he was a fool. Any man who has a woman who loves him, should bask in that love, because it can be taken away all too soon," Captain Murphy said, but his tone was gentle.

Joan looked into his eyes; at first she was going to snap a reply to him, but for the first time in her life she saw the sympathy of someone who had also suffered. It was not an emotion she expected to see in the eyes of the man she had thought her tormentor. "Who was she?" she asked, her tone not its usual sharp self.

"A girl named Florence," Captain Murphy said honestly. "She was to join me some years ago, but I had one more journey to do before the marriage could take place. In that month, she was ill, and I don't need to explain the sad end to my tale, do I?" he said with a small smile.

"No," Joan replied. She turned back to look out over the waves that were becoming calmer with every minute that passed. "I'm sorry for your loss," she said and, for the first time in her life, she meant the kind words.

"Thank you," Captain Murphy said, himself turning to face the ocean once more. "It was over ten years ago now; the memory does fade. How long have you been a widow?"

"Three years," Joan said quickly.

"You were but a child yourself when you married," Captain Murphy responded.

"Maybe, but the world is a harsh place; the quicker we learn that the better," Joan said, her voice hardly above the sound of the waves.

Captain Murphy looked at Joan when she said her words, but it had been almost as if she were speaking to herself. Her expression was one of someone who was lost. He had seen it before: families ridding themselves of troublesome relations, sending them to some far off island, hoping they would reform, remarry, or die, rather than come back home and have to be dealt with. It was something that always angered him; no one should be cast out, no matter what they had done.

He had quickly noticed Joan above the other passengers. Three sets of married couples, business people, a nun and a priest were the usual type filling his passenger quarters on a regular basis, but Joan was one of the relations being sent away; he was certain of it.

He was not one who usually singled out his guests as he had Joan, but something drew him to her. If she smiled more, and ate more come to that, she would be far prettier, but the frown was more common than the smile. He looked over the ocean and sighed; in two days his cargo would be unloaded and new cargo added; he would be back at sea and worrying about a young woman who terrified most of his men would have to be put to the back of his mind. He had a job to do, and he always did it well.

"I hope you find what you're looking for," he said gently, turning to Joan.

"I doubt it; I am more likely to find yellow fever," Joan said sharply, her weakness being covered up once more.

Captain Murphy smiled at her and, on impulse, took hold of her hand and bent to kiss it. He heard Joan's sharp intake of breath and smiled, his usual cheerful demeanour looking into her eyes as he let go of the hand. "It has been a pleasure, Lady Joan." He walked away, leaving Joan feeling shock, surprise and a warmth on her hand she had never felt before.

*

Joan left the gangplank, wanting to look back, but forcing herself to look forward. She had not seen Captain Murphy since their encounter earlier that morning and now they were in port and unloading. She had expected, hoped, that he would come to say goodbye; she was going to give him a piece of her mind for taking advantage of her like that. She could ruin his business if she let everyone know what type of man he was, taking advantage of widows in such a way.

Joan sighed to herself; she would do nothing of the sort. He had been one of the few people in her life who had shown some compassion towards her. The only other person had been her friend Frances, whom she had not deserved because she had treated Frances ill, but Joan had to lash out at someone, and Frances had been there and been a willing victim. Only once had Frances stood up to her and, because of it, Joan was starting this farce of a life.

She was greeted by a servant and escorted to a waiting carriage. She smiled at the standard of the carriage; at least her father had sent over enough funds that she would live in comfort.

*

Captain Murphy had purposely kept out of Joan's way. He had surprised himself at his actions and cursed himself for far longer. What did he think he was doing? He always behaved like the gentleman he was. He smiled;

he was so far beneath her notice, she would never consider him a gentleman. She had been a challenge to him when she had first come on board, but it was not many days before he had started to see some of the vulnerability behind her sharp and cutting remarks. His mother always used to say the eyes were the doors to the soul, and he often wondered on the voyage if anyone had ever truly looked into Lady Joan's eyes.

Wanting to comfort someone who had been hurt was something he could not allow himself to get entangled with; he was a sailor at heart and could never settle in one port. Florence had understood that and been willing to be an onboard wife. Lady Joan would never agree to that. He paused and then took one last drag on his cigarillo before throwing it overboard in disgust at himself. Since when had he started thinking of marriage to the most unsuitable woman he had ever met? Even if he could bear to stay on land, which he could not, she was still a termagant; no, he must be going soft, and the quicker they set sail the better.

*

John Wilson, First Mate on the Blackbird approached his Captain and best friend. He had watched Patrick Murphy over the last three weeks with hope. For the first time in ten years, Patrick seemed interested in a woman. John did not necessarily agree with his taste; he would not have been attracted to the sharp faced woman, but Patrick must be able to see something in her: he had not shown any interest since Florence. Oh, there had been women, but nothing that kept Patrick whistling throughout the day.

John had hoped Patrick would think of a reason to stay in port, but it had not happened, and they were minutes away from the order to set sail. It was time John interfered. He approached Patrick and gave him the list of cargo the hold was now bursting with.

"We have the cargo loaded, ready to drop off at Mumbai, and then its three weeks until Liverpool, unless…." John said, trying to be casual.

"Unless?" Patrick asked his friend, looking up from the lists he was checking.

"We could always leave you here and sail back for you after Mumbai?"

Patrick looked at John with a frown. "And why would I put you in charge of my ship?"

"Because you know I can handle her just as well as you can, and it will give you the opportunity to spend a week in the company of a Lady," Patrick said with a smirk.

Patrick raised an eyebrow. "I didn't know your middle name was Cupid."

"Really? And we have been friends these last twenty years," John responded.

"Thank you for the thought, but we will set sail as planned," Patrick replied, touched by the offer.

"Are you sure? You have been cheerful these last three weeks; if we're going to see the return of the grumpy Captain, I need to warn the men. Some may not be willing to go back to the old Captain Murphy," John said, jokingly, but he meant every word.

"Good God, I have been cheerful?" Patrick said horrified. "There must have been witchcraft at work."

"Some would say she was as sharp as a hag," John pushed.

Patrick looked at John sharply. "If any made comment in my hearing, they would receive nine lashes before they finished their words."

"Murph, go and find her; if nothing happens, you've wasted a week of your life, nothing more. Surely she's worth that?" John said seriously.

Patrick turned away from his friend. It was tempting to see her again; he had seen what she was beneath that exterior and was drawn to her because of it. He was not sure if he could do anything in a week. "What happens after the week?" he asked quietly.

"We are due back here in two months, surely she would wait," John said.

"I waited before; it didn't end well," Patrick said.

"I know," John said, resting his hand on Patrick's shoulder. John had seen the grief his friend had suffered. "It doesn't mean it would happen again. Look at Mary: she waits for me on every voyage we make; she says it makes for a perfect marriage: I set sail before she has time to get sick of me."

Patrick chuckled. "And I dock before I do the same!" He took a breath. "If you harm my ship in any way, I shall hunt you down, because I know you won't be stupid enough to return here if you do."

"Aye, aye, Captain!" John said with a smile.

"Good voyage, John. I'm off to visit a widow!" Patrick said, the smile emerging that would have won a thousand ladies if he had aimed it in their direction; fortunately for Lady Joan, she was to be the one who received it.

"Good luck, and I expect an engagement at least in a week!" John said, slapping his friend on his back.

The End

About the Author

I have had the fortune to live a dream. I've always wanting to write but, life got in the way as it so often does until a few years ago. Then a change in circumstance enabled me to do what I loved; sitting down to write. Now writing has taken over my life, holidays being based around research, so much so that no matter where we go, my long-suffering husband says 'And what connection to the Regency period has this building/town/garden got?'

I do appreciate it when readers get in touch, especially if they love the characters as much as I do. Those first few weeks after release is a trying time, I desperately want everyone to love my characters that take months and months of work to bring to life.

If you enjoy the books please would you take the time to write a review on Amazon? Reviews are vital for an author who is just starting out, although I admit to bad ones being crushing. Selfishly I want readers to love my stories!

I can be contacted for any comments you may have, via my website

www.audreyharrison.co.uk or

www.facebook.com/AudreyHarrisonAuthor

Novels by Audrey Harrison

Regency Romances
The Four Sisters' Series:-
Rosalind – Book 1
Annabelle – Book 2
Grace – Book 3
Eleanor – Book 4

The Inconvenient Trilogy:-
The Inconvenient Ward – Book 1
The Inconvenient Wife – Book 2
The Inconvenient Companion – Book 3

The Complicated Earl
The Unwilling Earl (Novella)

Other eras
A Very Modern Lord
Years Apart

About the Proof Reader

Joan fell in love with words at about 8 months of age and has been using them and correcting them ever since. She's had a 20-year career in U.S. Army public affairs spent mostly writing: speeches for Army generals, safety publications and videos, and has had one awesome book published, (italics, I'm on my kindle and can't get there) Every Day a New Adventure: Caregivers Look at Alzheimer's Disease, a really riveting and compelling look at five patients, including her own mother. It is available through Publishamerica.com. She also edits books because she loves correcting other people's use of language. What's to say? She's good at it. She lives in a small town near Atlanta, Georgia in the American South with one long-haired cat to whom she is allergic and her grandson to whom she is not. If you need her, you may reach her at oh1kelley@gmail.com.

Printed in Great Britain
by Amazon